Daniel Davis Wood teaches literature and history at the Ecole d'Humanité, Switzerland, where he lives with his wife and daughter. He was born in Sydney and studied in Boston and Edinburgh before completing a PhD in Literary Studies at the University of Melbourne. His literary criticism appears regularly in various journals and online at www.danieldaviswood.com.

BLOOD
and BONE

Daniel
DAVIS
WOOD

First published in Seizure by Xoum in 2014
Xoum Publishing
PO Box Q324, QVB Post Office,
NSW 1230, Australia

www.seizureonline.com
www.xoum.com.au

ISBN 978-1-922057-95-2 (print)
ISBN 978-1-921134-22-7 (digital)

Cataloguing-in-publication data is available from the National Library of Australia

Internal design and typesetting © Xoum Publishing 2014
Cover design by Zoë Sadokierski

Edited by Emily Stewart

Viva La Novella 2 was made possible through the generous support of

BLOOD
and BONE

Of course, you summon ghosts at your peril.
The sufferings of others can bleed into
your soul. You try to protect yourself.
Susan Sontag

PART I

Often I find myself wanting for words when I set out to say things about Rowan Scrymgeour. A dozen discarded notebooks contain the wreckage of earlier efforts, and fragments scribbled on receipts and napkins litter my desk like shrapnel from a blast. The problem is not that words escape me altogether. The problem is that they burst into babble the moment I try to commit them to the page. It's as if the soul of Scrymgeour himself refuses to abide containment in words and thwarts all my efforts to concentrate him into some expressible form. But I don't mean to begin with a writer's complaint so much as a concession to the inadequacy of writing. Every last word that follows from here is a word I have tortured out of myself. If what I have written sometimes warbles towards the inarticulate, that is the price exacted by torture and the price of articulating Scrymgeour at all.

What compels me to speak of Scrymgeour now is the

total, deceptive erasure of his complexities in the only other likeness of him in public view today. The statue was unveiled on June 18, 1971, outside the council chambers of the town of Jericho in the deserts of central Queensland. I have been there and I have seen it, twenty-two miles east of the site on which Scrymgeour built his homestead and a century after the settler was slaughtered while his dwelling was burned to the ground. Mounted atop a sandstone plinth in a weatherproof coat that licks at his heels, he stands beneath the scorching sun to gaze out over the western plains with the determined demeanour of the visionary pioneer. His deepsunk eyes should be shielded from view by a brow pinched into a squint by the glare, and his high cheekbones and tight, thin lips should have been warped by a scowl, but the certainty of the sculptor's mould has forgiven his every crudeness. It's likely that what suggested his features to whoever cast him in three dimensions was a scratched and faded ferrotype portrait taken in 1890, or one of the reproductions Scrymgeour published in broadsheet newspapers that year, and so it's possible that the flaws in the art say less about the sculptor's skills than about the shortcomings of his source. But the face in that portrait has haunted me for more than half my life, ever since my mother showed me a copy when I was a boy, and looking at it now I see that it undermines the statue's authority by clearly afflicting the settler with hardships missing from the bronze.

Rowan Scrymgeour glowers out from the sepia heatstruck and sweatstained, wearied and worn down, swarthy, savage, flyblown and bitter. Every last one of his fifty-odd years is etched into his weatherbeaten face. His short, choppy hair recedes across a scalp splotched over with blisters and moles, and bugbites and blemishes cascade from crow's feet and scatter his cheeks to slip under the fuzz of a scrubby beard. Not that he appears impoverished or in any way feeble and sapped of his strength. In a charcoal waistcoat, narrowed at the sides, and a white-collared shirt rounded out by broad shoulders, he projects in his posture enough self-assurance to distract from the shock of the scars on his skin. Tilting his head down just a notch while slightly lifting his line of sight, he meets the eye of the camera with a deep and penetrating glint. A grim wound curves down from temple to cheekbone, skirting the rim of his left eye socket, and beneath it the upward slash of a harelip twists his mouth into an involuntary sneer. His right shoulder slouches an inch below his left, the result of an injury that afflicted him with a lifelong limp, while his left hand reveals postaxial polydactyly as he clutches at the waif who has just flinched in front of him.

The name of the girl is Abigail. She is eleven years old or thereabouts. She has a weak, wiry frame wrapped in thin skin made ruddy by too much sun, and the same thin lips and deepsunk eyes as the man whose touch has caused her recoil. More notable, though, is the long, lank hair that hangs loose around those features, combed straight without any attempt at a braid or chignon, as well as the white gossamer gown with lace trimmings tarnished, despite its elegant cut, by threadbare sleeves and a stain at the waist. Having evidently dressed up for her portrait, and yet having failed to meet the standards of her time, the infelicities of her appearance hint at a life lived far beyond the presence of even one other woman. Hers was a youth spent with only her father for company, and he was the sort of man whose company was rarely tolerable. You can see it in the pressure of his fingers on her shoulder. He clasps her by the clavicle as if seizing a runaway dog by the scruff. He clasps her as if to stop her from fleeing like the son who turned his back on his father so many years before. I'm sure, of course, that neither of them thought much of this pose at the time. Knowing what I now know, however, I can't help but look back on that frozen clasp and see it as less a record of a fleeting touch and a flinch than a distillation of the entire existence this man and this girl shared out there in the desert.

When historians discuss what occurred at the Whangie and at scores of other homesteads like it, the word they most often favour is 'flashpoint'. When I stand in the dust where I know the Whangie once stood, I can't think of any word more appropriate.

'Flashpoint' evokes an explosive flare so intense, so violent, that it consumes every last vestige of life around it before consuming itself and flaming out in an instant. The desolate landscape here seems to have suffered exactly that sort of torment. Nineteen miles west of Jericho, a bend in the road to Julia Creek is the nearest sealed surfaced to where the Whangie was built. The site itself sits three miles further across a wasteland of white dust and chalk marl and skeletal scrub. Only animals now inhabit this place. Jack jumpers with gigantic jaws march across the earth on some unfathomable mission while the air comes to life with the whorls of insects and flies that pollute it like smog. Kite hawks dangle roadkill from talons as they haul themselves into the sky. Ravens swoop and skip over the dust to guzzle the entrails that drop to the ground.

Far back in the east behind me I can hear the rumble of an oncoming car and the distant whip of its passing by, and then I hear, from up ahead, the murmur of the Auchtermuchty River. Taking a few steps towards the murmur, the land this side of the water slopes off while the far bank eclipses the western horizon and soars upwards to form the Auchtermuchty Escarpment. The sudden rise marks the easternmost edge of the mountain ranges that ripple across the continent before smoothing out into the Great Sandy Desert. The churning water chews away at the rocky base of the rise as if the water itself has prised apart the earth and allowed sunblasted highlands to ascend in the west while suppressing the flatlands from here to the coast. Diverting from a course running southwest to north-east, from the Great Artesian Basin to the rainforests of Mackay, the river at this point hooks around in a horseshoe formation to carve out a sort of inland peninsula at the foot of the Auchtermuchty Escarpment. That peninsula, a half-mile long by a quarter-mile wide, was once known as the Auchtermuchty Bend, and the Bend was where Scrymgeour decided to build his little empire, the barn and the stable, the outhouse, the hitching-post and the cattle-pen, the wheatfield, and the clapboard shelter of the Whangie.

So many years after the events that obliterated his already precarious settlement and made this flashpoint a flashpoint, what first stirs my imagination is a vision of the cataclysm and its immediate aftermath. The slash and burn, the ambush and slaughter, and then the scattered corpses left to bloat beneath the sun. The leaking orifices calling out to swarms of insatiable insects and the bile and innards spilling from flesh and swelling the gullets of birds. But these images first stir the imagination because they are conjured up by the destitution of the Auchtermuchty Bend itself. Far more difficult to imagine is what made the Bend an appealing place, what led Scrymgeour first to look at it as a haven on which to stake a claim and then to resolve to defend his desolate claim to the death.

I can imagine him here on this blighted expanse of nothingness. I can hear his footsteps biting into the gravel with a limping plod and shuffle. I can see the shadow of a horse beside me, a darkness splayed across the white, and, turning, I can see the sorry beast all saddled up with lumber and bursting a cloud of flies with a snort and a twitch of the ears. Beside the horse is the man. He lurches forward, bent at the waist, and keeps his hands in the small of his back with one hand clasping the wrist of the other. He brushes past me, I imagine, as a hot wind whispers across the dust and whips it over the tops of our shoes. I can see flies crawling through the bristles of his beard. As he shuffles by me now I turn so he can't escape my sight and I watch him as he retreats from me and carries himself towards the escarpment. I imagine his jaw jutting out with every step he takes. I imagine those eyes scanning the ridge as it towers above him like a monstrous wave frozen the instant it crested. I wish I could imagine what he foresaw when he first set foot on this land. I watch the stomp and drag of those feet as Scrymgeour begins his descent to the river. He walks on, I think, like a man snared in vines, the vines of the empire he has come here to flee and yet whose reach he extends with each footfall he takes beyond its frontier.

Before the Whangie was wiped from the earth, set ablaze and reduced to charcoal and ash, it crouched in the shadow of the Auchtermuchty Escarpment like a cornered rodent raising its hackles against the encroach of a predator. This I can say for certain without imaginative exercise. Coastal tabloids commissioned no shortage of artists' renderings of the Whangie in the weeks after the ambush. For years after that they also reproduced the sole surviving ferrotype of the homestead taken just months before its destruction. It was a rickety hut, around four hundred square feet, cobbled together from slats of wood too thin to rest straight upon the foundations. The foundations were firm, jammed deep into the dust, leaving the land with scars that have survived there to this day. But the walls of the Whangie bent and bowed where planks of wood refused to sit flush, tilting the homestead towards the escarpment a little more each moment. From the outside it gave away nothing but four slanting sides and two vacant windows, a dead flat roof and a wraparound porch. The door and the window beside it both faced west with a view over the downhill slope to the river and across the water to the looming rise of rock. A cattle-pen extended southwest of the homestead, bound on the farthest two sides by the horseshoeing turn of the river and bound on the nearer sides by a timber fence whose two arms ran up from the water to converge near the corner of the porch. A small, sad wheatfield stretched out to the northwest, the inverse of the cattle-pen but bound by nothing and ragged at the edges. Between the wheatfield and the cattle-pen, flanking the barren path from the homestead down to the water's edge, a barn stacked with straw gave shelter to a huddle of chickens, a stunted stable secured enclosure for a horse or two, and a rude and no doubt filthy outhouse reeked of human waste. A hitching-post stood like a totem pole at the head of the path, equidistant from the northeastern corner of the cattle-pen and the southwestern corner of the porch around the homestead. The crawlspace under the porch sheltered a supply of driftwood and scrub, a supply replenished daily so that the flames in the fire pit on the far side of the hitching-post might never dwindle or die. Take a step onto the porch and over the kindling and take another step forward to enter the Whangie and you would have sent a pulse thundering through the place. The flimsy thing must have rattled in even the slightest breeze. Any presence in the homestead would have kept it in constant motion as even the smallest movement trembled it deeper into the dust.

I imagine that if there was a single, identifiable instant when the girl began to grasp the terrible reality of the life to be lived here, it was the instant the homestead fell still and trembled under only her tread. She had recently moved to the Whangie with her mother and father. Whenever more than one of them sought shelter in the homestead, the whereabouts of anyone moving was instantly known to the others. Her father's limping gait shuddered the Whangie with a succession of stuttered, maundering jolts. Her mother, moving with corseted poise, offered the walls of the Whangie a sort of atmospheric rumble that dimmed into silence only when the woman slowed. The girl herself, with featherweight steps, brought a percussive hum to the house like the barely audible grumble of an empty stomach. The day before stillness set over the Whangie, all three had sheltered beneath it. I imagine the white glow of sunlight piercing walls, spilling through gaps in wooden slats to cast shards of light across every surface, and I imagine the flies alighting on floorboards and zipping through the air and in and out the open door. The girl leans out the window from which she watches the roiling river. I imagine her father in the shade of the porch, stripping the chaff from a bale of wheat, and I imagine his wife on her way back from the barn, straight and steady as she proceeds up the path, carefully cupping the day's eggs in her hands while the hem of her long dress catches her heels. I imagine she steps onto the porch and sweeps past her husband to set foot inside the house. I imagine the way the eggs smash on the floor, their sickening splatter, and then the rumbling walls as the bewildered girl watches her mother stride past. The woman drags open a door and slips into the room forbidden to her and there, I imagine, she seizes a jar, twists off the lid, raises the glass to her lips and swallows a draught of formaldehyde.

The woman drops with a sudden thud that shudders the Whangie from top to bottom. The girl looks on in confusion as her father leaps to his feet and explodes into the house. His boots find the puddle of splattered eggs and kick the flies into a whirlwind. Before he can even reach his wife she is possessed by seizures that rock the building. He staggers from side to side towards her as if shocked off his feet by an earthquake. He disappears behind the door and, a minute later, the seizures stop and the house stills itself. After a heartbeat the sudden silence sets off a ringing in the ears of the girl, and a heartbeat after that she hears her father shouting her name and then shouting her into her quarters. Go to bed! he growls from within

the forbidden room. Close the door behind you! Take
yourself to sleep! She does not disobey him, although
the day has not yet reached dusk. She tiptoes through
the Whangie. The walls around her hum. She steps
past the door to the forbidden room and then enters
her own room to lower herself onto the white sheet
over the pile of straw that serves as her pitiful mat-
tress. There she watches the night settle in. The light
that penetrates the walls begins to flee the room.
When everything is dark and still she can hear her
father elsewhere. Once or twice a floorboard jitters as
he tries to contain the spasms of weeping. Once, too,
a floorboard thumps as he perhaps lifts and lets drop
his wife's hand. Then, deep in the night, he eases open
a creaking door and shambles out of the Whangie.

The girl is woken when dawn sprays daylight across
the walls around her. She lies there on the sheet on the
straw where she listens to her own breathing and then
strains for other sounds. When her eyes adjust to the
light she notices a human shadow on the floor nearby.
She sits upright on the straw to find her father standing in the doorway. At first he does not move. His
face, his bare arms, his shirt and trousers are stained
grey and white with dirt and dust. His entire body is
dogged by the stench of chemicals and bile. He sags
there against the doorframe, exhausted and breathing heavily through his nostrils, and then he meets
her eyes with those deepsunk eyes of his. Abigail, he

mutters. Come now. Come and say your farewells. He shuffles aside and waits for her to push herself up from the ground. She rises with stiff joints and stumbles towards him, then past him, and steals down the hallway with his feet at her heels while his limp creaks the house in her wake.

The woman now lies on a dining board too narrow to hold up the dress that spills over the sides and down to the floor and too short to support her legs between her ankles and her knees. Already the rising sun has flooded the homestead with heat. Already the flies whip around the room, mad with the warmth and the smell of dead meat, and mindlessly butt into the walls and the ceiling and into the girl and her father. The girl eases towards the body. The top half of her mother's dress has been stained yellow with some chaotic mixture of fluids. Only the face has been wiped clean. It does not remain clean for long. A fly alights on a cheek, then another alights beside it, and together they sit scrubbing their paws before again twirling upward into the air. At the sight of the flies the girl's father, behind her, steps forward. Very well, he says as he passes her and gathers up the fallen dress. Now I want you to stay here. I want you to not leave this house. He slides his arms beneath the body and lifts it from the dining board and passes by the girl again. She watches her mother's neck bend back over her father's forearm with hair spilling down to his belt.

As her father carries the corpse to the door, shuddering the homestead with every step, the girl watches her mother recede into the blinding day.

For the first time in the girl's new life at the Whangie, the homestead has succumbed to stasis. The air has not stopped writhing with flies but the sudden loss of human presence leaves all the floorboards and walls at rest. The girl hesitates at the door, perhaps anticipating her father's return, and shifts her weight from one foot to the other until she turns, but only slightly, to take in the dining board. She reaches out to it and gently runs a finger along its edge. I imagine she stands there a little longer, dwelling in murky thought, in some admixture of rage and confusion, before she raises her eyes from the board and spies the open door to the forbidden room beyond it. Even then, I imagine, she lingers awhile before she resolves to enter. She would not want to be caught in the act. She may not even truly want to see what that room looks like right now. With her father nowhere in sight, however, she carries herself through the rudimentary kitchen, past the door to the other bedroom, and towards the entrance to the private space where he prefers to spend his evenings. Her footsteps send tremors through the floor for a moment, but then the tremors cease when the girl takes a breath and slips through the door to where she knows she should not be.

The forbidden room is equal parts menagerie and

mortuary. A lopsided desk, splintering apart, is lost beneath a mountain of glass containers entombing an array of things long dead. An enormous tapeworm lies coiled in a jar. A baby crocodile in another jar sits submerged in preservative fluid. Snakes, dry and brittle, seem frozen in place in small wooden boxes with flat glass lids, and dozens of test tubes stopped with wax or gum or sometimes only wads of cotton imprison gigantic insects and worse. One is crammed tight with jack jumpers, another with locusts, a third with black spiders whose legs have drawn inwards the way burnt paper curls into ash. Two cockroaches, each the size of a man's thumb, are dead on their backs in a glass near the edge of the desk. A scorpion has gone limp nearby, lifeless with its pincers and its sting-tipped tail at rest on the glass pane beneath it. A small beaker, unstoppered, overflows with a swarm of dead hornets whose pinched faces and strict wings compete for space with their colossal thoraxes and barbs in a riot of yellow and black. In the thick of this mess, a broken microscope clings to the desktop. The rest of the desktop belongs to papers covered in handwritten notes and other specimens too small and too numerous to identify at only a glance.

I cannot imagine that the girl was shocked by what she discovered behind that door. Her father's private interests were no secret. While his amateur attempts at anatomy and taxonomy had been confined to the forbidden room, he had declared the room forbidden less to conceal his fascination with his specimens than to attempt to save them from damage. He often returned from Jericho with new jars and test tubes in hand and openly carried them into the room as his wife and daughter looked on. In any event, what captured the girl's attention when she entered the forbidden room was not the spectacle on the top of the desk but the dark wooden chest that sat at its base, a footstep in from the open door. Her eyes fall upon it after having passed over the specimens. She scans the floor for some trace of her mother's final moments and finds the chest right there at her feet with its brass latch fastened but left unlocked. The specimens may be spectacular but the wooden chest is intriguing and I imagine the girl imagining that hidden inside it is a new and outlandish specimen of some creature even more gripping than those left to lie out here in the open. I imagine her daze as she kneels to unfasten the latch and then heaves aloft the lid, and I imagine her suddenly hit by the smell not of death but of musty clothes unworn for many years.

The homestead around the girl remains still for now but it will not remain that way for long. Her father, outside, coughs away the dust that rises from the grave he has just filled in, then he sighs and turns and starts for the homestead as the girl reaches into the chest and takes out the white shirt and black coat on top.

She sets the shirt aside. She raises the coat in the air and lets it fall open, unfolding, until it assumes its full length. Its bottom half hits the ground with a slap. It is a thick oilskin, a man's riding coat, bigger and heavier than she can hold high with her small, scrawny arms. She crawls up from her knees, one foot to rise and one to balance, then she grips the coat tight in one hand while she slides the other hand into a sleeve. She cannot see her father now just outside the homestead and shambling towards the porch. She scrunches the sleeve back down into her armpit until she can see her fingers again, then she slides her first hand into the next sleeve and settles the great coat around her small shoulders. Huge cuffs swallow her fingers and lapels flap closed over her chest, but she has barely wrapped herself up in the coat before a step on the porch sends a shock through the Whangie and her father limps in through the front door. The coat clings to the girl as if it has been fashioned from tar. She has no time to wrench herself from it and fold it and set it back in the chest with the shirt on top, the lid closed, the latch refastened, the forbidden room abandoned and empty. The stuttering of her father's gait announces his impending arrival. The Whangie jolts with his every step and only settles back into stillness when he reaches the door beside the girl, eases it open, and enters.

Rowan Scrymgeour fixes his eyes on the girl and

watches her wilt beneath him. He takes a step towards her and with one polydactyl hand he reaches out to cup her chin and cradle her head and he guides her gaze to meet with his. He looks down at her a long time as he ponders her appearance. Dressed like this, she recalls for him the boy to whom he once offered that coat, the son who left that coat behind when he left his father's life. His breathing through the harelip makes a frightful hiss. That coat, he manages to mumble at last, that coat was not made to be worn by a girl, and then in a flash his fingers splay out and snap at her face with a smack that stings her cheek and summons tears that sting her eyes. Before she can even let out a cry he clasps a thumb across her lips, fingers at rest against her jawline, and warns her wordlessly not to whimper.

I imagine he did not spend a long time considering their situation before he did what he did next. I imagine that the day had brought with it a need to work and a need to eat which pressured him into a quick decision. Listen to me now, he says softly. If you intend to dress like a boy, you seem to me to be asking to work this farm like a boy. Then his hand falls away from her face and he seizes the coat by the collar and strips it off with a single swipe. The coat drops to the floor. His hand drops onto her shoulder. With a steady pressure there he turns her towards the door, sweeps her out of the room, and propels her through the homestead at a suddenly frantic pace. He brings her to a halt at the front door and the threshold to the wraparound porch. A white haze smothers the world outside. The girl peers up at her father to find him gazing down at her and then, without taking his eyes off her, he places his hand in the small of her back and thrusts her out into the war zone.

The dogs were the first to be put to death. The station servant, Baulie, called them together and bludgeoned each one with a short, sharp blow to the skull. He worked in darkness, far beyond earshot and out of view of the whites who had already slunk off to bed, and he worked in collaboration with the raiders who would slaughter the whites before sunrise. On October 25, 1857, half a dozen Jiman tribesmen swept through the Dawson River sheep station known as Hornet Bank. The men inside the cabin were killed where they slept or where they stood up to fight. The girls and women were ushered outside into the predawn dark. The eldest three women were raped by the Jiman, by men who had likely learned the trick from the settlers who first encountered the tribe, and then the white women and girls were put to death much like the dogs. When the sun emerged on the distant horizon, the men of the Jiman fled west with Baulie and left eleven bodies bleeding out behind them. Sylvester Fraser, fourteen years old, was the sole survivor of the massacre at Hornet Bank. He had been knocked unconscious by one of the Jiman and left for dead inside the house. When he came to, he raised the alarm that sent local settlers and the Native Policemen on a campaign of vengeance that would consume them for many decades to come.

The conflict had been building for years. In 1853, the superintendent of Rochedale station on the Upper Dawson was decapitated. After that, settlers along the river made sport of angering the tribesmen who occupied the surrounding bushland. They would load their firearms with pellets of salt and shoot the tribesmen with buckshot far too dispersed to end a life but just strong enough to sting the skin. The tribesmen responded with cattle theft and spears sent smashing through windows at night. In 1855, the Commissioner of Crown Lands for the District of Leichhardt reported that local settlers had whipped themselves into a state of unprecedented panic. Just after Christmas that year, three men were stabbed to death and a woman raped and strangled at the Mount Larcombe station near Gladstone. In 1856, two shepherds from Eurombah station, about three miles from Hornet Bank, quit and fled in fear of their lives. Another slit his own throat in order to avoid a more violent death and a fourth was found murdered before the year's end. Early in 1857, a large group of tribesmen set upon the station and, although local police dispelled them, they managed to maintain a permanent presence in the vicinity. In June, police attacked a tribal camp at the junction of the Dawson River and Palm Tree Creek and sent the tribesmen scattering through bushland in the area of Hornet Bank. Days later, by nightfall on June 15, the settlers there were convinced that an attack was imminent and requested immediate police assistance.

Assistance arrived at daybreak on June 16 and forced a retreat amongst the Jiman who had drawn within a few feet of the homestead. All of the livestock on the station were later found slain, two dozen cattle and a hundred sheep all gone to waste and rot, and so, in the monstrous words of one who was there, the frontiersmen met in solemn conclave and resolved to give the niggers a lesson. Local settlers slaughtered the first dozen tribesmen they found, none of whom had taken part in the thwarted raid, and then a station overseer killed another black man in cold blood after accusing him of stealing food from settlers and of suggesting that settlers had solicited Jiman women as prostitutes. In July, as many as a thousand warriors from dozens of different tribes across Queensland gathered together on Palm Tree Creek. The gathering was, by all accounts, a communal attempt at forging a military strategy, and military strategy was what brought Hornet Bank to ruin less than three months later. The Jiman specifically planned a predawn attack to be sure that their victims would be asleep. For weeks in advance they kept away from the homestead in the hope that their victims would let down their guard. They secretly liaised with Baulie to remove any obstacles in their path and, crucially, they held off their attack until Hornet Bank felt the absence of one particular settler who left home to spend a few days tending to business up north.

Billy Fraser was the eldest son of the patriarch of Hornet Bank and brother to the boy survivor. His voice was perhaps the loudest amongst those urging violence against the Jiman in the wake of the Rochedale murder, and his participation in later reprisals earned him a reputation for coldhearted cruelty. In theory, the Jiman would seem to have acted wisely in attacking Hornet Bank only after Billy Fraser had taken his leave of the station. In retrospect, however, that attack in his absence seems the greatest flaw in the Jiman strategy. The tribesmen failed to anticipate the unremitting, almost totalitarian ferocity with which Fraser would subsequently hunt and eradicate them. Their succession of assaults on the settlers gave Fraser a grudge they would come to regret. He received word of the massacre when he reached Ipswich and turned around immediately to tend to his traumatised brother. He ordered the Native Police to pursue the Jiman mercilessly and he demanded the death of every tribesman regardless of personal involvement in the bloodshed. He summoned a gang of fellow settlers and embarked on what historians of the massacre refer to as a series of dispersals. Best estimates suggest that he personally slaughtered at least one hundred and fifty tribesmen and more likely upwards of three hundred. Some were Jiman. Many were not. He killed them wherever he found them. He chased them down like beasts when he saw them at a distance while out droving cattle. He beat them to death on the spot when, in town, he passed them walking in the streets. He murdered every indigenous man he ever laid his eyes on, shooting and slashing his way through the tribes of southern Queensland over some twenty-five years, and in every instance he did so with the complicity of a justice system that blinded itself to his barbarian bloodlust. By 1880, the Jiman had been hunted into extinction and settlers had made inroads into the territory of tribes far beyond what was once Jiman land.

At the time of the massacre at Hornet Bank, Rowan Scrymgeour was the steward of a droving run from Townsville on the Queensland coast to Bourke in inland New South Wales. His route extended nine hundred miles from north to south and passed through the White Mountains, Marathon, Charleville, and Cunnamulla. He would follow that route up and down for sixty days at a stretch, thirty days each way, under contract by other cattlemen whose stock he would herd from high land to low land, from grazing ground to grazing ground, wherever rainfall and swollen rivers had made the earth most fertile. Sometime in the late 1850s, although I can't be sure exactly when or how, Scrymgeour met and forged an acquaintance with Billy Fraser. While I have been unable to find any correspondence which might directly demonstrate that the two men knew one another, their relationship has been noted in passing by some of their mutual associates. One of the broader responses to the massacre involved settlers forming a sort of network and collectively moving themselves farther westward. Over the decades following the Hornet Bank massacre, settlers enacted a more or less concerted seizure of the land at the eastern extremity of tribal territory. Their objective was to intimidate the inland tribes into yielding to the white advance. Offering support to their efforts was an officer in the Queensland Colonial Police Force who reportedly assisted Billy Fraser in his attacks against the Jiman and who later provided assistance to Scrymgeour in his work at the Whangie. So when Scrymgeour constructed the Whangie, four hundred miles west of the station at Hornet Bank, he wasn't just building a home for himself and his family. He was also extending one small front in a broader offensive coordinated by an alliance of settlers in outback Queensland and prosecuted against the indigenous peoples of the Australian interior.

The section to which he laid claim was gazetted in 1867 as settlers developed a trading route between the port of Rockhampton and the copper mines sunk near the town known today as Cloncurry. It's possible, even probable, that Scrymgeour spearheaded one of the dozens of Aboriginal massacres that scarred Queensland throughout the 1860s and 1870s. At Mailman's Gorge, just outside Aramac, twenty-five Aborigines were slaughtered in 1868. Although the settlers who took those lives remain unidentified, Mailman's Gorge would have been less than a day's ride from the Auchtermuchty Bend and settlers there were so thin on the ground that it seems to me unlikely that Scrymgeour could have remained uninvolved. It's not hard to imagine him leading or joining the raid on the tribal encampment in Mailman's Gorge while he traversed the northern leg of his droving run.

Since the Auchtermuchty Bend was only a little north of the midpoint of the run, the run divided almost evenly into a northern and a southern leg. Scrymgeour seems to have constructed the Whangie by purchasing materials at the end of each leg and then returning to the midpoint to assemble the homestead in piecemeal fashion. After droving cattle north to Townsville, he would return from there to the Bend with fresh supplies for the Whangie and then, after droving cattle south to Bourke, he would slouch back up to the Bend with more supplies before departing again for the north. One plank of wood at a time, one planted seed at a time, he pieced together what was supposed to be a new life for himself and what would eventually become the site of his bloody death. First he erected the cattle-pen fence, wooden posts driven deep in the dirt and connected by rungs of drift-wood, and with the fence in place he could build the Whangie while using his land as a waystation for the cattle under his care. Then he dug down into the moist clay beneath the baked earth, and there he sowed the grain that eventually straggled up into wheat. He did what he could to gouge runnels from the river so that a makeshift irrigation might soothe his fledgling crops. He hauled the Whangie into place over the course of five or six years. He laid the foundations on one visit and raised the frame on the next and then he slowly accreted the walls, the way a rising tide climbs up the shore, hammering a new rung of planks into place each time he returned to the site. He camped out in a swag under the stars while his horse snuffled asleep beside him and his cattle sighed the night away. Did he envision the Whangie as a station whose use he might offer to other drovers in exchange for a tariff? Did he hope to someday expand it with, perhaps, an oven, or a grain silo, or a horsedrawn coach offering settlers transit between Charleville and Jericho? Eventually, of course, he bartered or purchased livestock of his own, two dozen head of cattle to be used for both milking and breeding, and at some point he drove them into the cattle-pen and gave it over to them. For years he roamed his droving run to scrape together a living, and he used the back and forth of the run to invest his muscle and sweat in constructing what was, in equal measure, a shelter for a family and a fortress in a war. Knowing what I know now about his stance towards the tribesmen he would encounter, I don't believe that he would have fled a conflict like the one at Mailman's Gorge if he happened to have set out on the northern leg of his run and found himself facing a chance to participate. So determined was he to assert his hold on the land that he did not hesitate to brutalise anyone who might challenge him.

How did it occur to him that the greatest challenge to his claim now came from the girl with whom he shared his home? I have imagined a dozen ways in which realisation might have struck. It comes to him in the dead of night, with the corpse lying cold in the forbidden room, as he drags a spade down to the river to prepare a grave for his wife while his daughter lies in sleep. Or it comes to him at dawn, with the body splayed out on the dining board, while he stands at the feet of the sleeping girl and watches the rise and fall of her chest in the minutes before she wakes. Or it comes to him in the morning heat, with his wife sagging in his arms, when he orders the girl to stay in the house and carries the body outside and down to the grave through a throng of barking ravens. His hold on the land has so far been tenable only because he has been able to fall back on the funds he continues to bring in by droving. His droving run has so far been tenable only because his wife assumed responsibility for the maintenance of the land in his absence. The economics of his new situation are brutal. Without a wife to take care of the Whangie, he will have to forfeit his stewardship of the run. Without a run to generate income, he will have to shackle himself and his daughter to this farm and survive solely off its meagre produce. As long as she is there at the Whangie and yet remains unproductive, as long as her appetite depletes their scant resources without her labour replenishing them, she poses a challenge to his hold on the land. When he finds her idling in boys' clothing, then, the clothing offers him an excuse to order her to do what she will have to do anyway. If you intend to dress like a boy, he says, you seem to me to be asking to work this farm like a boy. Then with his hand in the small of her back he thrusts her out into the war zone in which he is determined to live.

Buckling beneath the burn of the sun, high and heavy overhead, the girl sets out to complete her boy's work and winces at the sting of each step she takes in waterlogged boots. There are crops and cattle to be sustained. After that, there is kindling to be collected, food to be prepared, clothing to be cleaned, and, amidst it all, a fire to be kept alive. I see the girl ambling uphill from the river with a bucket of water held in each hand. I can see, just over her shoulder, the soil still unsettled atop her mother's grave, the soil beneath which the body will whittle away to bones. I can see her dangling arms drawn taut by the weight of the water and I can see them peeling where the sun has turned her skin scarlet. She stops at the edge of the cattle-pen and sloshes the water into a trough. The spillage around her feet thickens the dust into mud. She has yet to develop a more careful technique. Later, I imagine, she battles against the door to the barn, then stumbles inside and recoils at the horrid stench of shit. The chicken coop reeks of droppings turned crusty underneath feathers and down. The girl breathes in and out through her mouth while she carefully plucks the eggs from the straw and places them into a basket. There are only a few to gather, too few, perhaps half a dozen, and once they have been collected the girl turns and kicks open the door and steps back into the glare. But this time, on her first attempt at this task, I can see the haste in her eyes and then I see what escapes her notice. As the door swings closed, it clips the edge of the basket she grapples under one arm. As the basket dips down at a slight angle, an egg tilts forward and rolls over the rim and plummets to the ground. The shell shatters against the marl. The liquid white and yolk splatter over the dust. The girl, I imagine, stands there transfixed and gapes at the egg for what seems an age. Then she raises her eyes from the ground to take in the Whangie at the top of the slope. Her father squats in shade at the edge of the wraparound porch. He rises to his feet when he finds her eyes on him. She tightens her grip on the basket of eggs and stands unmoving at the barn. She swallows hard and watches him and waits for him to approach. He drops down onto the slope. He limps downhill towards her. He does not take his eyes off her and then, drawing face to face with her until he towers over her, he comes to a standstill before her and terrifies her with a grimace and a sigh that hisses through the harelip.

Once again she wilts beneath him and stands there suffering the flies that worry her skin where it peels. I imagine she wants to explain that the breaking of the egg was an honest mistake but then, I imagine, she bites her tongue for fear of another slap to the face. Her father knows full well that she intended no malice. He also knows that the two of them out there cannot afford the luxury of mistakes and that, if he allows her to voice her excuses, she will likely allow herself to make mistakes in future. He searches, then, for a way to make known to her the price of an egg in a place where every sunrise brings with it the possibility of imminent starvation. He speaks to her with a rumble in his voice that scatters the buzzing flies between them. You will pay me in recompense, he says, for what you took from me just now. He glances up at the midday sun, and then he glances back down at the girl. Tomorrow morning, he says, you may take one egg for breakfast before you begin your work, but until then I'm afraid you must suffer through your hunger. Then he lapses into silence and waits for the girl to acknowledge his order.

At first she only stands observing the flies that prowl the surface of her scorched arms. After a moment she turns aside and, bowing her head, she lingers over the broken egg on the ground. It smells foul in the sweltering sun. More flies suck at the sickly yolk. From above she hears her father's voice. Abigail? he says. Do you hear me? She hears but she does not respond, or she responds but not with words. This punishment, as she sees it, is an injustice. It contains exactly the malice that was lacking in her mistake. She has already eaten nothing at all on this day that began with the death of her mother. To be forbidden from eating more leaves her with little to lose. She cannot respond to her father's malice in any meaningful way except to meet his malice with malice of her own. Resignation colours her eyes. She tilts the basket of eggs at an angle and then upends it completely. In the searing heat the shell and slop bubble into a pulpy mess across her father's feet. The mess seems to stare up at the girl as she stares down at it, and it even seems to anticipate her father's response to her malice as his hand drops onto her shoulder. As the fluid flows and coagulates around fragments of shell the colour of flesh, the mess foretells what the force of his fists will do overnight to her face.

During the years it took Scrymgeour to assemble the Whangie, he found a place for his dependants in basic lodgings in Rockhampton. My understanding is that, in his absence, the woman spent the weeks leading up to their relocation in what was diplomatically described to me as a nervous state. I can only speculate on how her nervousness might have shown itself. I do know that she kept a robust library which she was largely forced to sell off in advance of leaving the coast for the Whangie. I imagine she confined herself to her bedroom, kept herself behind closed doors, and spent a large portion of each day immersed in her beloved words. How else to divert her thoughts from the torment of her life in this place and the dissolution of the family who might have at least made it bearable? On those rare occasions when she emerged, I imagine, she carried a book in her hand and sat in a chair by a window but soon forgot about reading as she daydreamed gazing over the lively city outside. Could her son have been walking those streets just then, trying to find his way back to her and back to the home she kept in good order in the hope of his return? She rarely spoke aloud, I imagine, and I'm sure that when she did, during her last days in the city, her words took the form of platitudes intended to bury her daughter's anxieties under promises so idyllic that no one could possibly take them as truth. Father, mother, and daughter, she said, would all enjoy their new lives out west. They would wake each morning beside a river at the foot of a mighty mountain. The girl would be given her very own room in a house on a beautiful farm, and there they would all live simply and without worries in plenty of fresh air and sunshine.

It must have taken them about ten days to reach the Auchtermuchty Bend, or perhaps a little longer with a few days' rest in Emerald. Mother and daughter saddled together on a single mount. Scrymgeour scouted their route up ahead, a rider in the distance, all but dragging them through a land that grew more bleak, more austere, more forbidding with every lilt of the horse. I see the animals twitch their ears and swish their tails as the swarms of flies intensify, and I hear leather satchels full of water slapping hard against their sides. They loosen their hold on the bit as they plod further into the desert, and I notice the reins, once firm, now begin to slacken. I don't think I'm able to comprehend the tedium of the westward journey.

Uncountable hours of intolerable heat, the endless muttering of flies, and the warm breath of the inland wind. The groan of saddles, the clink of bridles, the monotonous thud of hooves newly shod. I can sketch the conditions of the ordeal but words alone are, I think, too weak to evoke the experience of it. To stop and dwell on its enormity, to attempt to internalise those conditions, is to reach out to grasp a horizon that recedes with every step towards it. And how to then convey the despair that surely descended upon mother and daughter when they reached their destination and for the first time saw the Whangie? Day after day through the desert only to arrive at that lopsided shack, a speck on the limitless landscape, shrunken beneath the Auchtermuchty Escarpment. No sense of grandeur or ceremony. No sense of comfort and no sense of relief. A couple of months, at most, before the Christmas of 1888, and this after owning the property for twenty years and postponing migration because the difficulty of raising their youngest child so far from the coastal cities would have made the woman's life torture whenever her husband was droving stock. Not that she would bear it for long even when he stayed home with her. From the moment of their arrival, she had perhaps six weeks left to live. I can't help but wonder if she felt, then and there, the first pangs of the compulsion to escape from this place which, in time, metastasised into a compulsion to end her life.

What I think I can imagine is the whiplash that followed in the next instant as the haze of despair blew out into panic. Scrymgeour settles his horse at the Whangie while his wife and daughter are still some distance from arrival. Before he dismounts he turns in the saddle and raises a hand that commands his wife to halt her horse on the spot. She tugs at the reins and the horse sways to a stop. She and the girl remain saddled there, a cloud of flies swirling around them, and they watch from a remove as Scrymgeour climbs down from his horse, lashes it to the hitching-post, and sets off at a lope towards the homestead. He bends at the waist to examine the dust, like a sleuth inspecting a trail of clues, with his rifle holstered to his good leg and a coiled whip looped to his belt. He steps up onto the wraparound porch. The homestead unleashes a groan. With one hand he eases open the door and then he carefully enters the Whangie and lets the door close behind him. As a silent spectator to this behaviour, behaviour disconcerting because unexplained, the woman feels her heart beating so powerfully that it threatens to burst right out of her chest. For a long time she and her daughter are left to sit and wait there on a horse breathing heavy in the heat of afternoon. At last the Whangie groans again, the door swings open, and her husband emerges. He drops from the porch into the dust and limps the distance towards her horse. When he reaches her, he takes the reins from her and turns to lead the horse to the hitching-post. As the horse ambles on, the woman looks down past its flanks to see what her husband saw in the dust. The earth is tattooed with human footprints. Many prints, not just a few, many dozens across the dust beneath her like choppy waves seen from the edge of a boat. A barefoot mob in frenzy must have surrounded the Whangie while the settlers who planned to make it their home were traversing the desert to reach it.

I imagine that the woman's heart refuses to stop its pounding, not least because the prints do not disappear as she approaches the homestead. Her husband extends a hand to help her dismount. As he then turns to help his daughter, the woman treads towards the Whangie only to see, from a stone's throw away, that the dusty prints extend to the door. She steps up onto the porch and feels the Whangie sigh beneath her weight, then she creaks open the door and enters the house with a languorous step and finds, inside, more footprints. She follows them throughout the house. Not a single room remains unmarked. Every crevice and every corner bears traces of many more people than were ever intended to enter this dwelling. For those people to not brush away their traces must have meant that they wanted the settlers to know that they had been there. For them to have been there in the absence of the settlers must have meant that they were already nearby when Scrymgeour laboured away, that they were watching and waiting until his labours brought the Whangie to completion, and that the work he thought had been solitary had in fact been conducted under surveillance. The settlers were watched wherever they went although, at first, the onlookers were nowhere to be seen.

Three times before her death, however, the woman saw them in the distance. The first sighting came when she was instructing the girl on how to make a loaf of bread. She and Scrymgeour had agreed that the girl should be taught minor chores to help keep the farm operative while her father was out droving. The girl had already learned to sweep floorboards and beat dust from bedsheets, and to boil river water and wash clothes in the fire that the family fed in perpetuity. Now, at the dining board, she was to prepare some dough for damper. While the girl moulded a sphere with her hands, her mother took the lull in the lesson to steal a glance out the window and noticed, right at the rim of the Auchtermuchty Escarpment, far above her husband in the wheatfield below, two silhouetted figures, apparently in conversation, looking down and then gesturing at the human speck beneath them. The woman flung open the door and fled to the field. The girl let the dough drop onto the board and raced to the door across unsteady ground. She stood at the threshold and there watched her mother snatch up her dress to lift the hem from her ankles as she stumbled downhill and called to her husband. He rose up straight where he had bent amidst the wheat. The woman reached him and gestured wildly towards the escarpment. When the girl glanced over to where her mother was pointing, she saw the two figures receding until obscured by the rocky rim. The woman stood in conversation with her husband a little longer, then slowly made her way back up the incline to the Whangie. She wore a look of dread when she returned to her daughter. She asked the girl if she had seen those men up there watching over the homestead. She asked, she said, because her husband told her that he had seen nothing and that what she saw was probably only a fantasy.

But the second sighting had nothing imaginary or hallucinatory about it, and even Scrymgeour himself could not dismiss or downplay the spectacle. The rocky rim again. The Auchtermuchty Escarpment at dusk. The setting sun gave the rise of land a scarlet halo. The woman had ventured down to the river to wring out a filthy rag. When she rose from where she knelt at the edge of the rushing water, she lifted her eyes to the rocky rim and saw, above her, a backlit behemoth shambling into the south. It appeared to have a dozen legs, a great belly that sagged to the ground, and sharp spines that stuck into the air and jangled back and forth as it strode across the land. Only when the woman noticed the sky shot over with carrion birds did she recognise it for what it actually was. Not a beast at all, but a band of hunters, five or six, each one using one hand to jab at the air with a spear while the other hand gripped and hauled the carcass of something freshly killed. The woman immediately turned from the river and prepared to run uphill to her husband, but she stayed where she stood when she saw him outside, at the edge of the porch, already staring up at what she herself had seen. She watched him watch the tribal procession as it struck a southward course along the rocky rim. Ignore them, he said when she voiced her fears of what might befall the family in the event of attack. This place will never become another Hornet Bank. Not unless they all want to lose their lives before the month is out. The risks for them are simply too great to justify another slaughter. But his reassurances proved useless. Her heart had been flayed by an anxiety that she was not able to quell.

That night she takes a bath in a hopeless effort to calm her riotous nerves. A wooden crate serves as a tub, placed beside the porch and filled with river water. She lowers herself into it and sits there well beyond nightfall until the water grows too cold to withstand and leaves her skin tensed and numb. When she returns to the house she is shivering. Perhaps she shivers with the chill. Without a word but without escaping the notice of her husband and daughter, she steps inside and gently sets a knife atop the dining board.

Perhaps she shivers with fear, with as much fear at the prospect of ending her life as at the prospect of living it. Did you take a bath with that thing? Scrymgeour asks, nodding towards the knife. You've no hope of fending off an army of spears with a weapon as sorry as that. Perhaps he genuinely misunderstands why his wife took that knife into the bathtub with her. Or perhaps he deliberately misconstrues it for the sake of his eavesdropping daughter. Either way, its significance does not escape the girl and not too many nights pass before she is the one to ease her pain by taking a bath and taking the same knife into the water with her.

Now that her father has dealt with her recent disobedience, now that he has channelled his fury into force, blisters burst up over her arms and blood encrusts her nostrils. A bruise swallows her left eye with swelling and blackens the entire left side of her face from her cheekbone down to her throat. She prods at the veins in her wrists with the tip of the tiny knife and, I imagine, her thoughts return to the third time her mother espied an onlooker. The sighting had been made at dawn, just as the girl and her mother set off to freshen the water for the cattle. As they followed the path to the river, two new figures appeared on the rocky rim above them. The girl's father was in the enclosure with the cows. One of the two figures gestured towards him. The girl and her mother stood frozen in place, but her mother called out her father's name. He looked to her across the cattle-pen and then to the Auchtermuchty Escarpment from which the wind carried a burst of distant laughter. A voice called out when he turned, the voice of perhaps a young boy who babbled in a tongue beyond all understanding, followed by another burst of laughter. The man stood staring up at the figures. The woman and the girl stood staring. The two figures exchanged words with each other, eliciting more laughter, before they departed on a westward course. The man looked across to his wife once more. The woman escorted the girl to the river and completed the rest of her work as usual, but at dusk that day, and this time without revealing her fears, she drowned her anxieties with formaldehyde and left her husband and daughter alone. Now, I imagine, the girl considers following the path her mother chose but she falters until a different path opens up to her. She need not drain the life from herself. She need only drain the life from the farm and waste and pillage every precious resource to bring the homestead to its knees. She heaves herself to her feet. A splish of water escapes the bath. She takes care not to drop the knife. She glances about in the outer dark and then, the soles of wet feet leaving a watery trail in the dust, she stumbles down to the cattle-pen where, with searching fingers, she seeks out the rope that holds the gate closed.

Perhaps my imagination tends towards melodrama. Perhaps my knowledge of later events misleads me into seeing the birth of an elaborate scheme where in fact there is nothing more to be seen than the girl's reflexive response to the cruelties of her father. What I know for certain, though, is that she decided to sever the rope on that gate rather than just prying it from the post that her father had twined it around. She could have loosened it with her fingers in far less time than she must have spent sawing through it with the knife. She didn't do that. She made a deliberate and purposeful effort to sever it and she did so, I think, because she wanted its frayed remains to suggest to her father that the chaos he would soon encounter was not the result of more human error but an unmistakable sabotage carried out with care.

The girl jumps awake, stretched out on the floor, when the thump of footsteps thunders through the boards beneath her. She had returned to the Whangie clutching her breath. When she stepped through the door she found her father standing over the dining board where, by lamplight, he was scribbling a note. He lifted his eyes from the page and watched her silently slip away to shut herself in her room. She lay on her straw bed. Her heart pounded against the wooden floor and throbbed a tension into her body that felt like a burr lodged in her chest. There she held herself tight and waited for her father to discover what she had done, and then she jumped awake, unaware she had fallen asleep, as his movements rattled and rumbled the homestead around her.

She sits up from where she had been lying on the ground. From outside comes the stamp of heavy feet on dust and, in the distance, the bleating of an animal in trauma. She hears the door creak open. She hears her father caught between a scream and a whisper as if his breath has been kicked from his body. No, he says, no, no, and then a stirrup jangles and something leather whacks against horsehide. No, he mutters, no, as a horse whinnies and then, with a spur, gallops away into darkness, away from the homestead, towards the distant bleating that has now billowed into a commotion amongst the cattle. A cracking whip unleashes a shriek through the night. It raises a louder grievance from the cows. The whip shrieks again, and again, as the girl's father grunts and haws and growls at them, and it shrieks once more before a rumble through the earth signifies the herd is on the move. The man shouts. The cows bellow. With the drover's whip lashing the air while he, on horseback, darts this way and that to make sure the beasts stay herded together, they trundle up towards the homestead and to the entrance to their enclosure. The shouting and bellowing continues a long time. When they wander astray the horse beats its hooves, the whip cracks wilder, and the shouts crescendo until the herd resumes its proper course. Eventually, though, the animals settle. The bellows dissolve into sulks and sighs. The horse hooves stamp on the marl as the cows amble into their pen, and then a hinge lets out a yelp as the girl's father closes the gate behind them.

Suddenly, far off in the darkness, the moan of a lone cow rises above the gurgle of the Auchtermuchty

River. The girl cannot see her father from here in this room with no windows, but surely she can envision the scowl that must have erupted when that sound struck his ears. Now the hooves of his horse begin to beat again, and he rides downhill at a canter towards the anguished animal. Another moan breaks out over the land, but deeper this time, more distressed and defensive. When it comes again it is a full-throated howl, a cry of agony more than anguish, followed not by another but by the scream of a human being under attack. The cow returns to moaning, once, twice, while the human sounds break apart into gasping, and then, worst of all, the cow lets out a bellow that falters just before reaching its pitch, rasps away to a suffering bawl, and at last cuts out into silence that lets the white noise of the river rush forth with a roar. The girl lies there on the floorboards, straining to hear something new above the bombast of her heart.

The front door crashes closed. The floorboards quake beneath her. Her father's ragged breathing drowns out all other sounds, his inhalations shredded by the splutters of a man who has been held underwater to within a heartbeat of death. The walls around her tilt as he braces himself against a beam on the other side of the house. He stands there, and he stands there, striving to catch his breath, until at last he swallows saliva and forces out a sigh. Then his footsteps down the hallway set the house to swaying. The girl's gaze falls on the gap between the floor and the door to her room. An orange light bleeds through the gap and seeps across the ground. The light grows stronger with every step that shudders the boards and finally comes to a flickering stop. She can see her father's feet cast in shadow and she can hear him snort, a shot of breath through his nose, where he stands on the other side of the door and lingers in hostile hesitation. She waits for him to open the door. He doesn't. As quickly as they strode towards her the shadowed feet retreat. The light recedes like a spent wave, her room slips back into darkness, and after her father limps away she catches the clunk of the lantern set down on the dining board and then, when she strains again, the insistent scratch of a quill across paper just on the other side of her wall. The river rumbles at the base of the slope and the horse, tethered somewhere outside, snorts and clanks its bridle with a shake of its head. The cows in their pen brush against one another and in the barn the chickens brood. There are no other sounds this night.

The girl feels her eyelids prised open by the white haze that thickens the dawn. Shafts of light penetrate every gap in the walls and ascend from jagged joints in the floorboards. She clambers to her feet. The Whangie hustles to life. She steels herself and waits for a response from elsewhere in the house. The Whangie relaxes into a motionless calm. She creaks the boards with tepid steps and reaches out to open the door, but when she slips into the guts of the house she finds it empty and without movement. To the front door and then onto the porch. The soaring escarpment is already lit up from catching the first light of day. The river below it slinks in the shadow thrown westward by the eastern slope on which the Whangie was built. On the northern side of the property, the wheatfield whitens in the glare of the rising sun. On the southern side, the cattle have scattered across the pen where they wait to be hit by the heat. In place of the severed rope the gate has been locked with a coiled whip. The day's first flies scuttle up and down the wooden beams supporting the shelter over the porch. The first ravens croak at each other down by the water's edge. The horse, like the man, is nowhere to be found.

The day has drawn close to noon, I imagine, when a thin plume of dust appears in the east and soars up and swithers on the horizon. The afternoon is blazing by the time the man returns to the Whangie and all the dust kicked up by his horse drifts back down to the desert. When the girl first catches sight of the plume she sits on the shaded porch and awaits the arrival of horse and rider. When she recognises the rider as her father, clad in a long brown slicker and a broad black hat, he and the horse together are more fatigued than she has ever known them to be. He is barely able to sit upright. He holds the reins limp in the fingers of one hand and lets his feet dangle free of the stirrups. He lolls in the saddle like a man afloat and swept hither and yon by invisible currents. The horse stumbles on, obedient but slow, one foot in front of the other but each hoof barely raised from the ground. With its mouth slung open and its loose lips flailing and frothing with foam, the man steers it past where the girl is seated and rides it to the side of the Whangie. The girl stands and follows but keeps her distance and watches her aching father dismount. The horse slouches against the homestead and falls to its knees, slumps to the ground, and drops its head in the dust.

The girl's father ignores her as if he has not even seen her standing nearby to watch him. He picks up a pail from beside the cattle-pen and limps down the path to the river. While he is gone the horse slaps its dry tongue around its dry mouth and scuffs its hooves against the dry earth. When he returns he squats by its head, places the pail of water before him, then grabs the horse by the muzzle and shoves the muzzle into the pail. Now as the horse laps at the water the man, still kneeling, raises his head to look up at the girl and allows her at last to see his face beneath the brim of his hat. A long gash, like a crescent moon, arcs around his left eye and stretches from his brow to his cheek. Dried black blood encrusts it while it oozes a mixture of fresh blood and white pus. It has none of the straightness of a slash from a blade. His flesh has been torn and peeled away or suddenly struck with a pressure so great that the skin has burst apart. He does not swipe at the flies that drink from the wound. He rises to his feet without unlocking his eyes from the girl and, in a voice made coarse in a throat blasted dry by the relentless dust of the desert, he whispers a single, quiet command.

Inside.

He limps inside behind her with his hand in the small of her back, again, to guide her where he wants her to go. I intend to sleep for now, he says, but then, before he leaves her and hides away in his room, he guides her to the dining board and steps around it himself so that the two of them face one another across it. The girl stares down at the board. He lifts something small from his belt and places it under her eyes. A portion of the severed rope. Then he lifts something else from his belt and places it on the board as well. The knife she dropped at the cattle-pen before she entered the house. He reaches out with a finger just beneath her chin and lifts her head up high enough for her to look at him when he speaks. Fortunately, he says, I lost only one animal last night when I might have lost my entire stock. The herd moved down to the water's edge. I rounded them up and drove them back, but one cow scared herself into the river. I tried to pull her out. Couldn't fight the current. She gave me this for my troubles, he says as he tilts forward the gashed side of his face. With her hoof. Hurt like the devil. What could I do? No good leaving her there to squeal all night or drown. I had to slit her throat. I judged it the only humane course of action. Now he lifts something more from the side of his belt and holds it up for her to see. A hunting knife with a twelve-inch blade and blood dried along its serrated edge. He drops his other hand from her chin to rest it on her shoulder. She does not lower her head but keeps her eyes on that blade. Still, he says, one cow is one cow and now you owe me for what you've taken, and releasing her shoulder he seizes her right hand and uses his thumb to bend her little finger all the way back to her wrist. He snaps it as if it were only a twig before the nerves even sing out in pain.

She unleashes the start of a harrowing scream that dies in her throat with a choke. She drops to her knees, her mouth full of saliva she cannot contain. Her father refuses to release her hand and wraps his fingers around her wrist to press it tight against the board. Her extended arm grows rigid as she huddles on the floor at his feet. Her trembling lips leave her chin clung to with strings of descending spittle. Listen to me, he says. She moans. He presses his thumb into the break in the bones and looms over her where she cowers. Listen to me. She sobs, heaving her breaths, and at last forces herself to look up at her father through eyes gone bleary and red. You took something from me, he says, and so, by rights, you must pay me for it. Now he takes the hunting knife and, steadying the blade against his thumb, he presses its teeth gently into the break. Do you understand me? You must pay me for what you have taken. If you do not have the means to pay, then you must expect me to take something from you in return. That is the way the world works. He presses the blade deeper still, deeper into the break in the bones but just gentle enough to not break the skin, and he narrows his eyes at the girl who can barely contain her torment. Do you understand me? he says. She nods, desperately, and slings saliva down the front of her clothes and over the floor beneath her. Good, he says. Now listen closely, because here is where I will show you compassion. He removes the blade from the break in the bones but keeps his thumb firmly in place. I will not take anything from you, he says. I will allow you to keep this finger. That does not mean it belongs to you. It belongs to me. It is mine to take whenever I please. Every moment I opt not to take it is a moment more you remain in my debt. Now. If you ever disobey me again, I will come to you to collect on that debt. If you ever slight me or trivialise the work we do here, or if you fail to treat my instructions with the appropriate gravity, I will come to you to collect on that debt. The next time you imperil our existence in this house, you will lose this finger. Am I understood?

She cries and forces a nod of the head. Immediately he releases her hand. He reaches into the front pocket of his shirt and removes a handkerchief which he tosses to her. Use this to bind your finger to the finger beside it, he says. Then take yourself outside to feed and water the cows and the chickens and water the plantation. I intend to sleep today. He turns and leaves her to cradle her injury and ambles through the homestead in the direction of his room. Do not enter this house once you have stepped outside, he says with his back to her. Do not wake me under any circumstances. Then he opens the door to his room and swings it closed behind him, and the house he just shook with his movements grows tranquil around the blubbering girl.

At this point, I feel the need to issue a confession. The more I try to imagine the life shared by this man and this girl, the more I worry that the way I imagine it is not even close to the way it was. As I attempt to account for the intractable animosity that I know developed between them, all I have to guide me is the bare outline of the moments at which it flared. Scrymgeour ordered his daughter to work the farm and he punished her harshly for her mistakes. Abigail released the cows from their pen and suffered the penance of a broken finger. That's what happened. Those are the facts. The details are all conjecture. I have no way of knowing for certain what either of them might have been thinking or exactly what moves they might have been plotting at any given moment. I mention this because, while focusing on daily life at the homestead, I have so far felt at liberty to speculate on the undocumented details of their time together. But now, as the settler and his daughter collide with the world beyond the Whangie, I feel my imagination dulled and constrained by a responsibility to historical truth.

The world comes to them in the form of a man, rotund and awkward on horseback, who first appears as a blip in the distance before sauntering into clearer view. A dozen ferrotypes have survived the years. An inflated stomach reined in by a belt fastened a notch too tight. Bushy brows over bright eyes and the leathery complexion of all men of his lot. Mutton-chops descend from beneath a uniformed cap and cover the jowls that jiggle with every horsebound swagger. I see the girl transfixed on the porch where she scrubs a sheet with river water while her father tends to crops down by the river's edge. The stranger rides towards the girl, all conviviality, with a twinkle in his eye and a grin that shrugs his handlebar moustache. Ernest Shadbolt was an officer in the rural affairs division of the Queensland Colonial Police Force. He was also the associate of Rowan Scrymgeour and Billy Fraser to whom I earlier alluded. In 1857, he was one of the first eastern settlers to join the reprisals against the Jiman after the massacre at Hornet Bank. In 1864, after joining the Colonial Police, he seems to have withdrawn from participating in the reprisals but not from offering protection to those who chose to remain active. According to reports housed today in the Queensland Public Records Office, Shadbolt was an official witness to the murders of no less than eleven Aboriginal men and women who suffered the misfortune of crossing paths with Billy Fraser. Those murders occurred between 1867 and 1875. It is telling enough that Shadbolt happened to enjoy Billy Fraser's company with such frequency during those years. More telling is that he apparently lacked the resources to deter or halt those murders, and to apprehend and charge Fraser for them, even though he was an officer of the law.

I do not know the exact circumstances under which Shadbolt first met Scrymgeour, although, with Billy Fraser as their mutual acquaintance, I think it's safe to assume that the reprisals against the Jiman brought them together. If that's true, then it's also safe to assume that Shadbolt and Scrymgeour had taken pains to remain acquainted in the decades following the earliest reprisals. I suspect they maintained contact on a reasonably regular basis while Scrymgeour stewarded his droving run. Since Shadbolt stationed himself in Charleville, on the southern arm of Scrymgeour's run, it would have been easy for Scrymgeour to meet with him four or five times each year. Sometimes I imagine that they were indebted enough to one another for Shadbolt to saddle up and join Scrymgeour on part of his journey with the cattle. I see them sharing a dying fire on a bitter winter's night, each man shivering beneath his swag while a gathering fog engulfs the animals lowing around them. Sometimes, though,

I imagine that Shadbolt and Scrymgeour were acquaintances only for the sake of convenience. Scrymgeour, at least, strikes me as the sort of man who placed no value on the companionship of others unless he could see some material gain in it. I suspect that Shadbolt possessed a similar spirit but concealed it behind a more affable façade. Perhaps, for Scrymgeour, Shadbolt was simply a valuable contact on the right side of the law who could be called on to provide support whenever support was needed. Perhaps, for Shadbolt, Scrymgeour was a contact of a comparable sort, an itinerant settler who could keep an eye on the land and offer a glimpse of what transpired beyond the eye of the law. Each man, involved in his own pursuits, turned to the other to seek assistance on occasion, but each also saw his pursuits as in some sense his warrant, his charge, to be quarantined from the other unless circumstances demanded disclosures and revelations. Working together in the murk between the warm handshake and the cold shoulder, either one would offer a helping hand on request but would also respond sharply and swiftly if the other imposed on his business.

It was by request that Shadbolt made his first visit to the Whangie on January 16, 1889, as he noted in the report he wrote upon his return to Charleville. I see him ride up to the girl on the porch while Scrymgeour works at the water's edge and I hear him laugh and offer the girl a friendly greeting. What's wrong, love? he says. Cat got your tongue? He wears an officer's uniform, the colour of smoke from head to toe, and halts his horse and leans out of the saddle to inspect the girl before doffing his cap. My word, he says with his baldness revealed. Silence, eh? What a change this is. Couldn't shut you up the last time you and me were together.

They were last together some seven years earlier when Shadbolt had paid a visit to the family in Rockhampton. They would be together this time for twenty-two days or nearly so. The night the cattle escaped from the pen, Scrymgeour had written a letter to Shadbolt and then ridden overnight to Jericho to arrange for its delivery. Earlier that day, he had discovered the remains of a ravaged chicken on the outskirts of the wheatfield as well as a set of hoofprints in the dirt around the barn. He needed to visit Townsville, ten days away on horseback, in search of supplies for dealing with one or more wild pigs. He asked Shadbolt to tend to the farm until he was able to return. I do not know enough about Shadbolt to imagine either his reasons for agreeing to Scrymgeour's request or the finer details of his tenancy. But judging from the reports that emerged after the fall of the Whangie, I do know enough to understand that he was always ambivalent about the existence of the homestead and that he bears some responsibility for its eventual destruction.

Inevitably, then, the thoughts he kept hidden from Scrymgeour have coloured what I imagine of this visit to the site. In the dispute between Scrymgeour and Abigail, I imagine that Shadbolt's sympathies lay mostly with the girl. I imagine he believed it unjust of her father to force her to live alongside him in the emptiness of the desert. I imagine he took pains to allow her some space and freedom while she was under his care. I imagine he even said things to her that would help her break free of the Whangie, or, at least, I cannot see how she alone would have decided to do what she eventually did unless he offered her some sort of advice and also, perhaps, encouragement.

Scrymgeour mounts his horse and strikes out for the northeast. The girl and her new custodian wander around the homestead, seared by the sun, as they wait for Scrymgeour to vanish beyond the horizon. They observe one another from an angle and a distance. While Shadbolt plans to tend to the farm capably if without true dedication, the girl slackens her pace as soon as her father drops out of sight and lingers on the porch from where she watches the stranger's movements. I see him turning, every so often, to take in his new surroundings and thinking, as I do, that the place might almost be placid, serene, if not for the dangers beyond the escarpment and the homestead dropped here as a bulwark against them. I see him as one of those men disturbed by quietude and pressured to combat the silence with sound, to speak aloud simply in order to bring some comfort to himself. He shakes his head wearily before he catches the eye of the girl. All this might be noble, he says, if it hadn't been built to be burned to the ground. He holds her eye for a moment to see if she understands, if she grasps the implication of his remarks. Then he frowns and turns away from her and strolls down the slope to the river while she stands and looks on.

She bakes some damper for dinner and shares it with Shadbolt outside. They sit together and warm themselves at the fire pit that cradles the undying flames. Shadbolt chews away at the bread, watching his horse twitch its ears where he has tethered it to the hitching-post, and then he bows his head and runs his fingers over his moustache and begins to speak to the girl again. I've been wondering since before I arrived here, he says, how much he's told you and how much he's withheld about your being out here together. But now I figure, for the next few weeks, it's you and me together here and it's best you know the situation because it's you who'll be watching my back. He sighs and bites at a wad of bread and chews it while he speaks. Very simple, really, when you boil it down to words. You've got a barn full of straw and you've got a fire here that I suppose, night and day, your father keeps burning. You know we've got our troubles with the natives? He narrows his eyes at her. The niggers, he says. Murderers. Kill us all if they had the chance. But they're back there over that hill, he says with a nod towards the escarpment, and so, y'see, if they set foot this side of it, your father and you and me are all under instructions to set this whole place alight. You take the fire to the barn and you use the straw to feed it. You burn the barn, you burn the house, you burn it all if there's any sign of the niggers anywhere near the buildings. Shadbolt swallows the last of his bread and slaps his hands together to brush away the flour. Thing is, he says, the smoke from the fire sends a signal to our men in Jericho. They'll see it. Soon as they see it, they'll come running, and they'll send a signal of their own to the next station, twenty miles further east, and the folks there'll come running as well. It's open war if the natives try any funny business this side of that river, y'see, and we've got a way of getting our forces together, quick, as soon as anything happens. It's that, he adds, it's that, that battalion just waiting to receive the signal, that's what keeps the natives where they belong. If it was just you and your pa out here alone with nobody back east to back you up, you'd be gone by now. Bones is what you'd be. What fixes the natives in their place is knowing there's more men all ready set to fight. Y'see? But I'm sorry, he says, I am sorry that you were brought into the middle of it all without even being asked, without even being told anything about the goings-on. It's not right. It's not right.

The next day the girl retreats to the porch and stretches out on her stomach just as the sun slips behind the escarpment. A moment passes before Shadbolt takes a seat beside her to watch the sky, blazed orange, devoured by darkness and stars. A shame, he says, a shame, watching you out here like I did today. He keeps his voice low in a way that seems appropriate for the dusk. You do good work, no doubt about that. But work like that shouldn't be there for you to do. We all told your pa, before he moved you out here, that he oughtn't to be bringing others into this, all this waste, this nothing. You without friends, without I don't know what. Without dances, without amusements, without anything you'd find anyplace else. What do you do here these days but work? And work for what? No wonder you're restless. A girl your age. He shakes his head and sighs and stretches out his legs so they hang over the edge of the porch. He pauses long enough to suggest that he has something important to say. When the girl glances aside at him he raises a hand in which he reveals a tiny hardback volume. I found some of these in the house, he says, but my guess is you're not yet able to read. Am I right? He arches an eyebrow. Actually, he says, my guess is that if you know these storybooks at all it's because your ma read them out loud to you. Am I right? She turns away from him and looks back out at the sunset. Tell you what, he says as he sets the book down on the porch and places a gentle hand on her shoulder. I'll do you a trade. You tell me what happened to your ma. You tell me where she's gone, you tell me what you saw. You do that and I'll read you a story tonight, and tomorrow I'll show you how to read something yourself. Now doesn't that sound like a deal?

The river runs along the base of the slope with a sound like an endless hush.

Shadbolt hopefully watches the girl. The girl, lying down, shifts her weight on the porch, shifts onto her elbows and then pushes herself up to sit upright beside him. She casts him a glance before she looks down at the porch with a sigh.

Mother, she whispers. She decided she didn't want to be here any more.

The following day the Whangie is set upon by words. Shadbolt writes them on slips of paper torn from a notebook and nails them to doors, walls, and posts. He writes BARN and nails the word to the barn. He writes COW beneath a sketch of a cow and nails the word to the cattle-pen. He uses the toe of his boot to write FIRE in the dust near the pit and he uses the tip of a knife to carve the word BATH into the side of the tub. He takes certain lighthearted liberties. He nails the word CHOOKS to the chicken coop. He nails the word SHIT to the outhouse. There is danger underpinning all this. No doubt Scrymgeour would not appreciate the gift of literacy offered to a girl he has committed to labour. Then again, in time, Shadbolt will return to the Whangie and speak to Scrymgeour using words more numerous and more dangerous than these labels on the visible world. He shows the girl how the sounds of words she already knows correspond to the letters he has scrawled in ink. He teaches her how to glance at these symbols and call them into the air with her tongue. He allows her some time to read each morning while he takes it upon himself to complete a portion of her chores. In return, of course, she must read aloud and remain within his earshot. He appreciates the way her voice displaces the silence of their isolation and he is grateful, now, to at last be able to hear a voice aside from his own.

The words disappear when Scrymgeour returns. He announces his journey across the land before he emerges from beyond the horizon. He brings with him the clanking of iron like a felon dragging a ball and chain. The moment the girl hears the clamour she sets about tearing the words from where they have been put on display. She rips each slip of paper from each of the nails and casts them into the fire. She kicks at the word FIRE to erase it from the dust. She turns the bathtub around so that the word carved into its side is pressed against the edge of the homestead. Shadbolt stands back as a spectator and watches on, bemused and troubled, as the girl conceals or destroys every trace of the amity they shared these past three weeks. He remains bemused and troubled as Scrymgeour approaches and slowly reveals the source of all that clanking. Half a dozen pairs of iron jaws hang down the sides of Scrymgeour's horse. They swing from chains that jangle in discord as the horse trudges on to the Whangie.

Shadbolt, I imagine, curses to himself in disbelief. He stands at the corner of the porch and there awaits Scrymgeour without taking his eyes off the traps. When Scrymgeour rides in close enough for Shadbolt to see his face, he dismounts the horse and gently leads it to the hitching-post. Shadbolt follows. All this? he says. All this for one pig?

Scrymgeour lashes his horse to the hitching-post and sets about unchaining the traps. That pig is a danger to us, he says. In the long run it's a danger as great as any native you'd care to name. He lets one set of iron jaws drop to the ground with a clatter that kicks up a cloud of dust. We can't afford to stand idle, he says, and wait to find out what sort of damage that pig might like to cause us. A second set of jaws drops into the dust at his feet.

You want a solution to pigs, says Shadbolt, you get yourself some poison. Throw it on a bit of meat and wake up in the morning with all your troubles gone. I thought that's what you had in mind when you said you wanted to solve this thing. But this, all this? This is too much. He gestures at the trap Scrymgeour has just unchained from the horse. These things aren't made for pigs, he says. They're made for grizzly bears.

They're fit enough for dingoes, Scrymgeour growls at Shadbolt. They're taken to market to be sold to men whose flocks diminish overnight. He heaves the trap off the horse, lets it drop with a clank, and sets to work on the next. The problem with poison, he says, is that, in time, it runs out. Suppose I bought poison, or used some of the poison I already own, and the pig didn't take the bait. What then? Buy more poison? Throw good money after bad? I can't afford that any more than I can afford idleness. I especially can't afford it if I'm plagued by more pigs in future. He glances at Shadbolt over the top of the horse as he unpicks the chains braided into the harness. I will not tolerate any threats to my campaigns, he says. Human, native, or otherwise.

Shadbolt spent one more night at the Whangie after helping Scrymgeour set the traps. One by one the two men hauled the traps down to the chicken coop, the wheatfield, and the vegetable patch in the fallow soil between the wheat and the river. Together they laid the traps on the ground and slowly forced open the iron jaws to lock them firmly in place. By the time they finished the job, six sets of rusted teeth were waiting to bite wherever a feral pig might be disposed to forage or hunt for food. Shadbolt departed at dawn and as soon as he was on his way, I imagine, a menacing air returned to the Whangie where the girl was alone once again with her father.

She wakes to the sound of an alien shriek, a wheezing squeal from off in the distance, and the Whangie suddenly rattles around her as her heart pounds away in her chest. Before she can even rise from the ground her father is out the door and loping into the pale dawn. For more than a week now her father has woken to find the jaws of the traps untouched and unfed, poised to snap shut but entirely empty. For more than a week now he has woken to find the hoof prints of pigs anywhere but where he wants them to be. At the far end of the vegetable patch, their paltry crop of lettuce has been uprooted. Along the periphery of the cattle-pen, he found two sets of prints overlapping. The girl looked on as these morning discoveries stoked his anger. At first he doubted the capabilities of his own trapping system. He fished a piece of driftwood from beneath the porch and hobbled around to each trap to use the wood to set them all off. Trap after trap chomped the driftwood down to a nub of splintery prickles. At last he resolved to use a lure. I can see the rancour in his eyes as he seizes a chicken and snaps its neck with a twist of his arm. I can see the rage in his posture as he hacks into the breast and rips out the gizzard and distributes the meat to the traps amidst a flurry of flies. He resolves to stay awake all night to wait for the pig to take the bait. The girl takes herself to bed after dark and falls asleep in an instant. Now the shrieking wakes her and she stumbles out of her room and out onto the porch where she finds her father jostling down the slope, already close to the chicken coop, and then only a foot away from a ferocious boar as big as the girl herself.

The animal's right hind leg is clamped in the jaws of a trap that has torn through coarse hair, bitten through bone, and severed the limb so badly that blood flows like water across the iron and down the length of the chain. The desperate boar uses its two forelegs to try to stand upright and scrabbles for purchase with its free hind leg but only scrapes up a curtain of dust. It raises its head to the sky and opens its mouth and unleashes another unearthly screech, a high-pitched yowl, and reveals its sharp teeth and massive curled tusks as it turns and huffs at the man nearby. It staggers towards him with its head lowered as if it intends to charge at him, but its lagging leg allows it only to paw at the dust before it drops to the ground in exhaustion. It falls silent for a moment. The girl gingerly steps down from the porch. Her father, below her, has not moved. He turns slightly to look at her and then turns back to the pig. She hadn't realised, until now, that he had his rifle with him. He raises the gun and places the barrel right beside the animal's head. The pig bellows at him again with foam at its mouth and blood on its teeth. Before the man pulls the trigger, though, he hesitates, or stops himself. The pig sways its head back and forth but does not move its body. The girl watches her father lower the gun to his side. He takes a step back from the pig and squats down to rest the gun on the ground. With one hand he reaches around behind his back and then rises to his full height and holds his whip in that hand so as to let the weapon uncoil. Its tip does a nimble dance across the dusty uppers of his boots.

He raises the butt of the whip high over his head and, after a flick of the wrist to twirl the tail twice in the air, he jolts himself forward and back with a cracking lash at the belly of the boar. The girl jerks aside with a cringe. He jolts again, his arm thrust out, as if summoning all the strength within him and channelling it into the whip in his hand, and he opens up welts across the pig's torso and along the length of its snout and its neck. The girl watches on in horror as the pig decays under the wailing whip. Her father lashes out and the pig kicks madly at nothing and bites at the air. Her father lashes out and the pig's left eye explodes from its socket in a burst of blood. Her father lashes out and the pig bites into its own trapped leg, exposing the flesh and tearing through tendons, in a desperate bid to break free of the iron jaws. Her father could not have been sure that a single bullet would properly crack the animal's skull and he wasn't willing to spare the expense of two bullets or possibly more. That's what he will tell the girl later. Now, though, he lashes out again at the pig and strips away its ears until they hang from its head only by the hair. He criss-crosses its snout with slits until he reduces it to a frayed and bleeding rump. He whips at the flailing penis until the member has been severed and then, when he is satisfied that the pig would not survive a moment in the wild even if it could withstand what he inflicted on it, he lashes the whip at the animal's throat until the skin withers away into a strip of pulp and finally splits apart. The pig gurgles up a throatful of blood in the dust and falls forward with trembling nerves, kicking its hooves as if running through an open field, and then, at last, it lets out a groan as the life leaks out of its broken body.

A warm wind rushes across the Auchtermuchty Bend with the steady rise of the sun and matches the murmur of the river to the west. The girl stands there feeling her blood thump a drumbeat through her body while her father hunches over, heaving, breathless, gulping down the morning air to bring himself to a state of calm. He spits out a gob of saliva and scrapes at the blood sloshed up and down his arms. He turns and stares at the girl wordlessly and almost dumbfounded as if he had not quite registered her presence before. Then he glances back at the pig and then surveys the sky overhead, the rising sun, and at last he drops his whip, kneels beside the carcass, and takes his hunting knife from his belt. Go stoke the fire, he calls up to the girl. She does not move. She watches him shove the blade of the knife into the hole in the throat of the boar so that it might serve as a handle with which he can drag the animal uphill. Listen to me, he says when he glances uphill and finds that she has not obeyed him. I want you to stoke the fire. I want you to do it *now*.

With a fistful of straw on the flaming embers of the fire that raged the night before, the girl brings a blaze back into the pit. She feeds the fire the driftwood and scrub stored under the wraparound porch. She encourages it with a steady supply of bark and kindling and watches it return to life with a rise and fall and a pirouette in the wind. Her father lets out a frustrated grunt from somewhere just behind her. She turns. He stumbles up the slope now cradling the pig the way he had cradled his wife when he carried her down to her grave. He rubs his eyes against his shoulders and sways his head like a listless cow, persecuted by the flies that assail him where he is covered in the blood of the boar. When he reaches the Whangie he drops the carcass into the wooden bathtub. He leaps onto the porch and hurries into the house. The walls rock around violently while he rummages inside. He emerges with his white bedsheets. He flaps them open over the bathtub and lets them drift down to cover the pig. Blood seeps through and stains the white. Flies attack where it pools. The girl looks on in horror as her father again takes his hunting knife, kneels at the side of the bath, and slides his hands under the sheets and sets to work. The sound of skin shredding like fabric. The sound of bones splitting and tendons snapping as they are forced to give up their grip. Every so often he peeks under the sheets to satisfy himself that his butchery is true. The flies flood into the space he opens. He lets the sheets resettle and continues with the carving.

The fire crackles high and hot by the time he returns his knife to his belt and rises up from his knees. He bends and seizes the edge of the bathtub and drags it across the dust, twenty or thirty feet, to where the girl stands at the edge of the pit. He hacks out a mouthful of phlegm and swallows what he can't spit. She watches flies scramble over the bedsheets and watches the sheets writhe with flies underneath. Listen to me, her father says. His skin, his clothes, and even his boots are all clotted with blood drying firm in the sun. I want you to stew this meat. Do not do anything else today. Leave all your other chores to me. Just make sure this meat is stewed. He draws a deep breath, then lets it out slowly. Make a stew of this pig, he says, and I will take it as repayment for the cow you took from me. Cook it well and it will feed us for a week or more and then, he says, and then I will consider your debt repaid in full. He glances at the fire and spits into it and watches his spit sizzle up into steam. Then he turns and strips off his shirt and begins his descent to the river.

The girl retrieves two iron pots from a cupboard inside the house and takes them back outside to set them on top of the fire. Then, as if peeling a bandage away from a savage wound, she pinches the corners of the sheets and pulls them back from the mound of raw flesh in the tub. Hundreds of flies burst into the air on currents of unbearable stench. The girl gags, turns aside, swishes her arms at the carcass to keep the flies away. I can see that the moisture and colour has drained out of the meat. I can see the meat browning and hardening in the sun without being even close to the flames. I can see that the girl's thrashing is useless, that even as she frightens flies with her arms a hundred more flies swirl around in their wake, and I can hear their tremendous droning, their buzzing as if the air itself hums with electricity. The girl scrunches her eyes closed and reaches blindly for the bathtub. Her fingertips brush over the desiccation she refuses to look at. Chunks of pure meat cut clean with the knife.

Ragged clusters of offal and veins torn in fistfuls from the bloody bones. She knows she should open her eyes. She knows that the meat cannot all be stewed. She knows he expects her to stew only the good meat, and first to sort the good from the bad.

She forces herself to look. Now she can see patches of hairy hide all mixed in with the flesh, and what she cannot see she can imagine, the lice and the parasites buried deep in the mess of rotting organs. She knows that the cow she lost was far more valuable than this pig and she knows that her father's new arrangement is a minor show of kindness. She knows his kindness will be honoured and her debt will be repaid only if she does the job properly and sets two bowls of hot stew on the dining board at dusk. Whether she wants to service the debt and allow her father the reconciliation he seeks is altogether another matter. She grabs a clump of flesh, warm and wet in her fingers, and throws it into a pot where it sizzles loud enough to drown out the droning flies. She looks over her shoulder, down to the river, where her naked father wades in the water and scrubs the blood from his skin. Then she quickly returns to the pig, seizing as much of the meat as she can and hurling it into the pot.

That night at the dining board, I imagine, the stew she sets before her father looks like something a dog would refuse. He has completed all the day's work and stomps inside at sundown. He braces himself at the dining board and stands there breathing hard. The girl places two bowls of stew on the board, two bowls as if she intends to eat alongside him, and hears his breathing slow when he sees what she has done. He peers into the bowl. Chunks of meat in thick brown jelly congeal beneath his nose. Strands of hair and shards of bone protrude from the half-cooked mess and dead flies float in the stagnant liquid. He does not raise his eyes from the bowl. He does not touch the spoon beside it. He sharpens his breathing through his harelip and stands there, still, with his hands on the edge of the board.

I'm not sure that I can look at him here and see him as a man infuriated by her. He does not raise his eyes from the bowl but he does not seem enraged so much as simply exhausted. Something slowly crawls across the dining board towards him, through the empty space between his bowl and hers, until it comes to rest beside his spoon. It is the girl's hand. She twitches her little finger, healed at an angle where he broke it, as if she intends to offer it to him. He forces out a snort of laughter, a burst of air through the nostrils to signal his incredulity, then he shakes his head to himself and presses his own hands hard against the board to push himself away from it. He turns and starts for the forbidden room. When he reaches the door he pauses before he swings it open. He turns back, just slightly, and looks at the girl and hovers there as if about to speak.

This is where I fear my grip on Rowan Scrymgeour falters. In earlier drafts of these pages I gave him a line of dialogue here, a question he asks of his daughter. In earlier drafts he squinted off into empty space and, more to himself than to her, he wondered aloud at what point she decided to declare herself his enemy. In earlier drafts I even delved into his thoughts as he scoured his memory to isolate the precise moment at which she had irrevocably alienated herself from him. But no such attempts at precision of thought have been woven into this version of his life because I have come to recognise the futility they entail. All I know for certain is that he pauses at the door to the forbidden room and then turns back to look at the girl. He says nothing to her and I cannot sense, I can only guess, the thoughts that might have welled up within him as he stood there watching her.

Despite the savage temper the girl has brought out in her father, I know that he was, at bottom, a supremely patient man. He may seem impatient and easily angered from moment to moment or day to day, but he held within himself the patience to suffer and outlast any antagonism from any opponent for any length of time. This is what the girl is too young to have learned about her father. This is what I impose on him, having learned what I learned about his early years. He has no intention of leaving this land and he has the infinite patience required to withstand her efforts at brinkmanship. He will die at the Whangie sooner than leave it and I'm sure that if she destroyed every last means of sustenance he would eat his own daughter down to her bones just to maintain his hold on the land for one more godforsaken day. He knows that he will outlast her here, he knows it without ever doubting it, and when I look at him looking at her with that weariness upon him I think I glimpse this knowledge, this ironclad certainty, beneath the emotions that shimmer and fade across the surface of his eyes. He does not think of what he knows. He does not need to think of it. His knowledge of what his future entails need not manifest as thought. He carries it with him in every cavern and recess of his soul. He carries it with him as the very foundation of his being in the world. He will win this contest even if it requires the destruction of the girl. He looks at her like a man for whom that knowledge is a fact of life, a truth so plain it doesn't warrant even the slightest discussion. He looks at her like a man who knows that she too will someday possess this knowledge if only he can summon the patience to wait for it to come to her.

When she wakes in the morning she finds him clean and clothed at the dining board and awaiting her arrival. Get dressed, he says when he sees her. I have some new chores for you to complete. With those words he opens up another front in their hostilities. Starvation is his weapon once again. He leads her down to the barn. Halfway to the river she sees that he has dragged the remains of the pig downhill. Ravens perched on the bones gobble down clods of gristle and meat. He opens the barn door and ushers her inside. Chickens cluck and tumble outside as a blast of musty air assaults her. Enormous bundles of straw crowd against the rear wall. The other two walls, where the chickens roost on railings, are caked in white and grey streaks of shit. Judging from last night's meal, he says, you have developed an affection for filth. That makes me very relieved. You can collect a pail of water and clean all the filth from this barn before you begin the rest of your chores. Every last little flake of birdshit is to be washed away.

She refuses to obey. He must have known she would. She flees the barn and coughs the rancid air from her throat, then looks up at him and waits for him to raise his hand to her. He doesn't. Just as if she had obeyed him, he sets about doing his own day's work. She sits on the porch and watches him until he returns to the house at dusk. Now he makes his strategy clear. He throws a pot in the fire pit and prepares a loaf of damper. He breaks the bread when it is ready and splits it, steaming, into halves. He sits in the dust on this lukewarm night and eats outside within reach of the fire. The girl looks on. He eats one half of the loaf of damper, then he starts on the other. When the entire loaf is gone he rises to his feet and dusts himself off and limps back to the Whangie. Until your labours bear fruit, he says as he passes by her, you will not eat again and you have my word on that.

The next day is much the same. She wakes with an angry stomach. He reminds her that the barn needs cleaning and then he ushers her into the stables and instructs her to clean them as well. Horse shit sits in darkened corners. Spiders scramble across the walls. The girl refuses to clean the barn. Her father sets about his own daily duties. She watches him, seething and starving at once, until he returns to the house at dusk. A frying pan on the fire. Two eggs alongside a flask of fresh milk. This time, when he passes by, he insists on his earlier warning. You're a foolish girl, he says. You will starve and I will let you.

On the third day she wakes to the same alien shriek that shattered the dawn three days earlier. She finds her father already outside by the time she escapes from the house. The trap at the edge of the wheatfield has captured another pig. The new pig is somewhat smaller than the first and, without tusks, it is much less dangerous. The girl watches her father lunge with his knife and slit its throat with a single swipe. He drags it up the slope, stokes the fire himself, butchers and dresses the pig, and prepares to stew the meat. He instructs the girl to clean the barn and the stables as well as the troughs for the cattle. She refuses. He gorges himself on meat. She tries to settle her hunger pangs by downing a mouthful of river water. She vomits up thin strings of bile. She cannot sleep that night. She writhes with the agony of one whose stomach is slowly eating itself.

When she forces herself out of bed in the morning, she finds a pail and fills it with water and finds a handful of rags and starts cleaning the barn, the stables, the troughs for the cattle. She works all day without rest. At dusk her father prepares another loaf of damper. Good work, he says. I'm pleased. He takes his hunting knife and uses it to slice off half an inch of bread. He hands her the flimsy slice and watches disgust creep into her eyes. She seems to be on the verge of hurling the bread to the ground. He knows she won't do it. She's too hungry for such stunts. She raises the corner of the bread to her mouth and nibbles at it before she shoves the whole slice in at once. He stands over her and watches her chew and swallow. Good, he says when the bread is gone and she looks up at him with a hunger for more. You can have more tomorrow, he says. After you've finished cleaning the outhouse.

She enters the outhouse at daybreak. She does not intend to clean it. She shuts herself inside and suffers the stench of human waste pooling in a shallow pit until she hears her father clatter out of the Whangie and amble into the wheatfield. She dips a pail into the pit and scoops out a gallon of liquid filth. She hurries back uphill to the Whangie and, with her tattered rags in hand, she enters the bedroom that belonged to her parents and now belongs to her father alone. A pile of straw for a bed and still no bedsheets clean enough to be returned to their proper use. She stands before a wall and rests the pail on the ground. Then she holds her breath against the terrible stench and dips the rags into the mess and, with great angry arcs of her arm, she raises up the dripping rags to smear on the wall, in shit, the word SHIT.

When he discovers the word, I imagine, he stands there for a long time trying to divine its significance. He grasps its meaning clearly enough, being a man of literacy, but he cannot grasp how the word might have come to the girl who scrawled it there. The shit has seeped into the cracks and fibres of the wood and has drawn a horde of flies inside. At the very least the word warns him that the girl has learned, or has been taught, how to read and write.

He collects a large pot and a chopping board before he leaves the house. He stokes the fire with driftwood and scrub and leaves the board beside the pit. He takes the pot to the river and fills it with water and then, on his way back to the fire, he makes a detour to the chicken coop inside the gabbling barn. He emerges with the pot of water in one hand and a plump hen in the crook of his spare arm. He rests the pot on the fire, squeezing a cluck from the bird, and then of a sudden he holds the bird tight and seizes its head with his free hand to snap its neck with a crack. He trembles, tensing himself, as the chicken in its death throes rampages against his chest. When it settles he holds it upside down by the legs and slaps it onto the ground. He squats before it and strips it bare, calmly and methodically extracting the feathers from the carcass. He is conscious, now, of the girl who stands in silence nearby, watching him from her vantage point on the wraparound porch. He rests the naked bird on the chopping board and dismembers it with his knife. He lets the blood dribble into the pit and then he casts the chunks of raw meat into the pot of boiling water.

I cannot imagine that he felt no pain when he did what he did next. I imagine, however, that he was a man accustomed to absorbing the pains he felt and able to inflict pain on himself to advance some broader strategy. He absorbed the pain of dragging those supplies across the desert to build the Whangie. He absorbed the pain of a life of poverty to maintain control of his homestead. So he passes the girl and strides into the house and soon emerges with each hand holding half a dozen of the books that once belonged to his wife. Without a word he marches around his daughter and returns himself to the fire and before the girl can cry out in dissent he feeds all the books to the flames.

She screams. He knew she would. The pages curl and blacken and wither away into ash. He sits in the dust and watches the fire while waiting for her to silence her sorrow. Eventually she crumbles into a snivelling mess and glares at him from a distance through red-rimmed eyes. He reaches for the pot in the fire pit and empties the boiling water. He waits for the boiled chicken to cool and then tears the moist flesh from the bones with his teeth. He tosses the stripped bones into the pit and devours the chicken, piece by piece, until all the meat is gone. He sits back and watches the dancing flames. He can hear the girl still snivelling nearby. Do you want to know why I did it? he says without turning away from the fire. The last of the books has long since charred and disintegrated into the dust.

Black ash from the burnt pages soars upwards and drifts through the air as an evening wind kicks up an eddy of soot and smoke. I did it, he says, because you have proven yourself to be an uncivilised child. The word, the *written* word, is one of the greatest triumphs of our civilisation, and yet you enter my house and you debase that triumph by using words for utterly uncivilised ends. For that reason, he says, I do not believe you deserve to have access to words at all. Nor, I should add, do you deserve access to my house. He rises and dusts himself off, and glances around until he finds her sitting behind him on the hard earth with her back against one of the thick posts that support the cattle-pen fence. You're welcome to sleep inside tonight if you're willing to take the room you defaced. That room will be your room from this moment forward. If that doesn't suit you, he says, be thankful it's not too cold out here. Or not yet, at any rate. Then he turns his back on her and returns to the empty homestead. He closes the door gently behind him as the gloaming of late dusk turns into dark.

It's possible that he failed to consider what she might do outside on her own. It's possible that he gave no thought to where she might be inclined to seek shelter and sleep away the night. She had grown accustomed to sleeping on nothing but straw and so she made her way down to the bales stocked in the barn. It's possible that he did think of this but then banished the thought because he did not know that the girl had acquired new knowledge during his absence in Townsville. That knowledge now returns to her as she eases open the door to the barn and prepares to make a bed of the straw. I see some trace of her father spring to life inside her here. When she sets her eyes on the straw it awakens a formidable patience. A minute or two is what it will take to gather up an armful of straw and cast it out onto the river. To gather up so many more, one after another until the barn is barren, she knows she will need the better part of the night. She has the luxury of eight hours until the new day dawns.

Her father finds her curled up inside the barn at sunrise. The door yawns open like the mouth of a vast and empty cavern. The girl is not asleep. Stray straw is scattered across the floor. He steps out of the doorway and looks down the slope to the river. The downhill path is strewn with straw as well. He turns back to the girl and feels his mouth fall open. His voice, forced out, is a whisper. Downriver? he says. The girl says not a word. You threw all our straw downriver?

He cannot stand her silence. He bursts into the barn and seizes her throat and drags her, choking, outside and uphill. It's possible that he is wondering how she could have known or guessed the purpose of the straw. It's more likely, though, that he is panicked by a sudden vision of downriver tribesmen spotting the straw float-ing past, watching the fuel for the warning signal swirling around on the water, and knowing that they may now strike at the Whangie without the risk of great resistance. Damn you! he bellows. Damn you! First you defile my house and then you risk its destruction! She claws at his six strangling fingers but he digs them deeper into her throat. He limps uphill with the girl in his grip. She jostles up and down in the dust as his arm rises and dips with each slouching step. He suddenly lifts her off the ground and slams her against the door of the outhouse. You want shit? he grumbles. He leans in close to her. The harelip and stubble and those deepsunk eyes. The cheekbones and the blanched red skin and the purple scar lancing the edge of his eye. You want defilement? He flings open the outhouse door and throws her into the rickety shack and slams the door shut behind her. You want it, so take it. It's yours.

Shadow and stench so strong she can barely see or breathe. She gasps for what little clean air she can find. A squeak at the door as her father fastens a rope to the handle outside. His crunching footsteps encircle the outhouse as he uncoils the rope around it. He hitches the end of the rope to the knot at the door and pauses outside to speak to the girl. You'll stay here, he says, until I decide I need you again. He tests the resilience of the rope with a rattle at the door before she hears the crunch of his footsteps, loud and then beginning to fade, as he ambles downhill and leaves her behind and alone in the dark.

I want to stay here with her now. Knowing what I know about what is going to happen, I feel moved to keep myself as confined as she must have been. What transpired next, what her father did, is something from which I prefer to remain distant. I worry that to throw myself into the mind of that man right now would be to invite complicity in what he is about to do. Safer for the soul to not stray too close, to cleave to the girl and make some virtue of this confined space and these four walls.

As the sun rises over the Auchtermuchty Bend it bombards the outhouse with a suffocating heat. A sickening warmth and stench steams up from the pit of waste. The girl, imprisoned, shrieks and howls until her throat is raw and slams her fist against the door until her knuckles bleed. She gags as dehydration descends and gags again when foam flecks her lips and draws the flies into her mouth. Lice chew away at her scalp. Horseflies suck blood from her knees and from the soles of her feet. Clusters of maggots pulsate at the edge of the pit. She slithers down onto her stomach to press her lips into the gap at the bottom of the outhouse door. She can drink in the outside air through the gap, but only if she lies prone. She forces herself to lie prone all day. When the sun reaches its zenith and the heat extracts sweat from every pore in her skin, she closes her eyes and breathes through the gap as steadily as she is able.

Night is nearly here, she knows, when a cool breeze brushes against her lips and sweeps away some of the stench. At dusk she hears the approach of her father's footsteps and crawls back from the door. He gives the door a rattle as he limps on past, but only to check that the rope is secure, and slowly makes his way back uphill to the Whangie. Darkness falls after that and brings with it a chill that penetrates the gaps in the outhouse walls to bite at the girl's extremities. She shivers at the elbows and knees and judders at the jaw. She curls into the foetal position to combat the cramps in her empty stomach. She moans when the cramps grow too intense for her to sleep them off. She lies there in the putrid air, tears trailing down from her eyes, and prepares to suffer the agony of every moment until dawn and beyond.

My guess is that midnight has come and gone when she catches the crunch of a footstep somewhere close by. She draws her breath and holds it in and strains to hear the sound again. There is no silence despite the solitude. At the top of the slope the embers of the fire pop and hiss. The chickens brood in the coop downhill while the cattle and horses shift and sigh. A steady wind rustles the wheat. The river churns into its banks. Yet just barely audible above these sounds comes the whisper of movement over gravel and dust. She swallows hard and strains again to hear whatever she can. Footsteps, unmistakable now, draw closer to the outhouse, but they move with a quiet and careful stealth in place of her father's arrhythmic hobble. Whoever is out there in the darkness approaches the outhouse, a foot in the dust on the other side of the door, and then proceeds almost inaudibly up towards the homestead.

The girl struggles to hear their movements above the militant thump of her heart. What she hears next is a sudden meshing of disparate sounds that I cannot faithfully detail. The scraping shank of metal on metal. The wet churn of flesh torn from flesh and the chock of snapping bone. A horrified pause before an intake of breath and then, so close to the girl on the ground that she could touch this person if not for the outhouse wall, a scream gurgles up from the depths of a human body in unendurable pain. A gasp and a grunt as the screamer struggles to subdue the sound. A helpless whimper and thud as the body slams into the hardened earth, and then the animal wheezing of someone slipping into shock.

She hears a muffled rumble spilling from the Whangie the way a growl of thunder escapes from distant clouds. She hears the door burst open and then she hears her father's scattershot footsteps draw near. She hears him descending the slope. She hears him freeze halfway. She hears his stunned silence fill up with the desperate rasps and tremors of a body convulsing in the dust. She hears the pitiless lock and load of a rifle brought to state. She hears her father's footsteps retreat and then she hears his voice ring out across the whole expanse of the Auchtermuchty Bend.

Show yourselves! he bellows into the void around him. Cowards in the shadows! You have me out-numbered! I am already beaten! Now show yourselves to me!

She hears the panting and the convulsions continue as her father's words spill into the wordless night. She hears him take a step, and hesitate, then carefully set off into the dark. She hears his unmistakable gait traverse the property from end to end. She hears him at the wheatfield and she hears him amongst the cattle. She hears him, at last, return to the path. She hears the panting as the convulsions beside her grow louder and more desperate as the minutes pass. She hears her father's footsteps slow but still approaching. She hears the clank of a chain dragged across the marl and she hears the clanking intensify as her father treads closer and closer. She hears, just barely, the lone voice of what sounds like a boy. She hears him mumble beneath his breath a string of words she doesn't know. Then she hears him raise his voice, stammering because he is trembling while trying to speak, and then the smack of a boot against flesh beats the boy into silence and sends him sprawling beneath the man.

She hears another sound now, a sort of whistled wail, then a grunt of summoned strength before the screaming slash of the whip. She hears a spooked horse beat its hooves against the earth and she hears an excruciating howl guttering out into a groan and she hears the wail of the whip again before another slash. She saw her father charge that whip with all his strength when he slaughtered that pig and I'm sure she envisions him now preparing to do it again, drawing in breath so deep he might draw in all the world around him. She hears stumbling movements, a flailing, a slump and a wail as the whip strikes again, a jangle of iron jaws, a chain scuttled over the ground. She hears the whip fall silent. She hears the ripping of fabric. She hears the muddled complaints of a speaker suddenly gagged. She hears the panting and gagging dissolve into pathetic cries, the same teary sobs that had overcome her when she watched the burning of her mother's books. She hears the cries choked off, strangled into a glottal groan, and in place of the cracking whip she hears the creak of a whip pulled tense and the spasms of a body fighting for breath.

She hears the body fall forward, hard, and hears gravel spit at the outhouse wall as the death throes kick up a pillar of dust. She hears, in a moment, the onrush of a nighttime quiet that stings her ears. She hears the slackening of the whip and a cough from her father as the dust begins to settle. She hears him standing there awhile, breathing heavy without moving, then she hears him spit up a gob of phlegm before he heads downhill to the barn.

A moment later she hears him straining back uphill, dragging something immense behind him. She hears it bump along the ground all the way up to the Whangie. She hears her father descend the slope and grunt again when he returns to the outhouse. She hears him grab at the motionless body and she hears the scrape and ding of iron drawn across solid earth. She hears her father battle with the body when he reaches the top of the slope. She hears him muddling around, dragging the corpse and struggling with what sounds like rope rattling its spool. Then she hears things she can't possibly picture. A drawn-out cry from her father as if he were trying to heave an immovable rock. The whine of fraying rope as it rubs against creaking wood, followed by another cry and heave. The clap of wood on wood. A sigh of exhausted aggression. The stillness that follows her father's retreat into the Whangie and, at first light, the cackled conversation of carrion birds who have stumbled upon a prize.

Daylight trickles into the outhouse. It stirs up the stench of excrement and awakens the flies that adore it. Soon enough the footsteps outside limp downhill from the homestead. Fingers pick at the rope affixed to the outhouse door. The footsteps encircle the outhouse again as her father unwinds the cords. She leans against the door, waiting for him to offer release, and when he swings the door open she tumbles outside as though diving into what must feel like a pool of cool air and harsh light. Her eyes need time to adjust to the day. Only slowly does the blinding white peel back to reveal the outhouse and cattle-pen, the Whangie above, and the dark form of her father before her.

I imagine she cannot resist surveying the scene to piece together the events of the night just gone. Her attention darts immediately to the homestead atop the slope and the hitching-post beside it. A larger, longer wooden beam has been roped fast to the post, rising a good ten feet in the air, and strung up with rope at the point of the beam are the sagging remains of a bloodied boy. He is black as charcoal and has been stripped nude. He cannot be older than thirteen years. He bears the raw pink streaks of lacerations across his chest. With his head dangling down and to one side, he shows deep gouges in his throat as if he has been garrotted. Clotted blood streaks his curly hair and bone and muscle spill from where his left leg has been severed just below the knee. He is bound to the wood like some heretic at the pyre, although his weight, and the weight of the black birds on his shoulders, bends the beam forward with enough flexibility for the corpse to loll in the breeze.

The girl, I imagine, is speechless. She looks to her father in unspeakable terror. What she finds, however, is a man struck speechless in turn as he looks back at his daughter. He stares at the girl beneath him. He stares long and intently enough for her to divert her thoughts from the boy and to wonder, just briefly, what her father is staring at. She glances down at her clothes. Dirt and streaks of human filth have stained her elbows and shoulders and the sides of her thin white dress. That's all she sees at first until another stain catches her eye. She is bleeding, or she has been bleeding, or at least she has been splashed with blood. Blood seeps through the fabric that falls between her legs. Her father cannot take his eyes off it. This blood, more than any other right now, is the blood that changes his world. It reminds him, I imagine, that the girl might sometimes dress like a boy and might even work the farm like a boy, but he cannot force the girl to live a boy's life at all.

PART II

I was fourteen years old when I first beheld Rowan Scrymgeour and learned a little of the life he led. I needed a story to tell at school for some project I can no longer recall. My mother retrieved a stash of pictures from a closet and pulled out the newspaper facsimile of the portrait of the settler and his daughter. I took the portrait to school the next day along with the story my mother told me. My great-great-great-grandfather was a frontiersman in colonial Queensland, I said. He came to Australia from England, he lived in the desert with his daughter and a few dozen other people, and, on the very day his long-lost son stepped back into his life, he died when the settlement he founded was attacked by tribal warriors.

I let Scrymgeour fall from my thoughts after that. The next time I saw him and heard about him, I was a man of twenty-six years. I had just returned to Australia after two years abroad in Boston and four more spent in Edinburgh. My parents had sold my childhood home some weeks before I arrived. They were in the middle of moving when my plane touched down in Sydney. I helped them pack away their belongings and that was how I rediscovered the portrait of the man and the girl. This time, when I pressed her for it, my mother offered a much more detailed account of their lives, and that account sent me in search of further details which altogether inform what I have written here.

My mother and father were married in 1972. My father is English by birth, but with strong family ties to Australia, and my mother, an American, has maintained a fascination with all things English for as long as I can remember. Although she never received a formal education beyond the age of sixteen, I have heard her speak passionately and knowledgeably about diverse aspects of English history from the Battle of Trafalgar to the Wars of the Roses, from the fate of Anne Boleyn to the rise of Margaret Thatcher. She is not a researcher by profession. She is not driven to understand a particular event or individual from every possible angle and in comprehensive detail. But whenever something captures her imagination, she will relentlessly and scrupulously gather as many facts as possible until she can see more than just the bones of the story beneath it. When she and my father became engaged in 1971, she spent a summer trying to unearth the background of her family-to-be. She had expected to find a trace of the convict stain, she told me, but what she actually found was a history in its own way more unsettling.

My father was born in Southend-on-Sea, forty miles east of London, in 1953. In 1969, at the peak of the 'ten pound pom' migration program, he persuaded his parents to move their impoverished family to Australia where they could make a fresh bid for prosperity. His father, my grandfather, was born in Lewes, Sussex, in 1916. He had started his family late in life, at thirty-eight years of age, after he and my grandmother lost a succession of children in childbirth, and I think that was why he saw something appealing about spending his later years on the sun-dappled harbour of Sydney. He was also the one who first sparked my father's desire to emigrate. In the winter cold of 1967 or 1968, he passed down to his son some rumours of a family connection to the former colony of New South Wales. Those rumours had come to him from his mother, a British nurse who had returned to Lewes from the Western Front after falling pregnant to an Australian soldier she met during service in Belgium. It was through that soldier that my mother was able to trace my father's lineage to Scrymgeour, and it is through Scrymgeour that I can identify exactly the place and date of my family's arrival on Australian soil. Rowan and Emmeline Scrymgeour disembarked the migrant ship *Mary Pleasants* at Moreton Bay, near Brisbane, on August 8, 1857.

In December 1971, six months after the statue of Scrymgeour had been unveiled in Jericho, my mother discovered that Abigail Scrymgeour was still alive at age ninety-three. A newspaper article on the unveiling mentioned that Abigail had declined to comment when approached by local reporters. My mother sent her a letter in care of the newspaper offices, explaining the family connection and requesting a face-to-face meeting, and in early 1972 the old woman sent a cordial reply including a current address. Abigail Scrymgeour, my mother learned, lived a self-sufficient but frugal life in a miner's cottage in Lutwyche, a suburb of Brisbane beleaguered by the ubiquitous damp of unbroken humidity, and she held in her possession a newspaper reprint of a portrait of herself and her long-dead father. What Abigail also possessed, as my mother learned when she accepted an invitation to visit, was a memory of her father not blunted by the passage of eighty-two years, and it is through her, with my mother as interlocutor, that I received the outlines of the life of Rowan Scrymgeour. The battle between the girl and her father, from the release of the cows to the breaking of the finger and the war of attrition that followed, was conveyed to my mother by the old woman who was once the girl in question. The portrait was sent to my mother in 1977, after Abigail died at age ninety-eight, and that's how it eventually came to fall into my hands.

The girl in the portrait is not gifted with any features I would describe as pretty. She is a tomboy, stick thin and glaring into the camera with hard eyes, a set jaw, and a posture of aggressive defiance. Yet with long, unbraided hair drooping down around her gaunt face, and with the first swell of breasts and widening hips accentuated by a dress a size too small, it is clear that the girl has recently taken her first steps into womanhood. As her father stands behind her with that possessive hand on her shoulder, I can't resist revisiting his thoughts on her new femininity. He made them increasingly explicit in the months before he prepared her to stand for that portrait, to pose for posterity. With the coming of his daughter's maturity they entered a tacit stalemate. Although she could no longer be forced to perform the labours of a boy, Scrymgeour did not see catastrophe when he looked at his daughter now. Instead he saw an unexpected opportunity to decisively strengthen his hold on the Auchtermuchty Bend, and schemes and strategies started to flourish as he resolved not to let it go to waste.

A letter from Scrymgeour to John Montague, the postmaster-general of Jericho, resides today in the Queensland State Archives as part of a collection of correspondence pertaining to land tenure after the colony's separation from New South Wales in 1859. I am even now startled and perturbed by the voice that appears on the page. The overwrought intellectualism, feigned and forced, is not something I had at first expected from a settler of Scrymgeour's social standing and yet, somehow, it is exactly what I should have expected from a man eternally convinced of his superiority to his lowly situation. I reproduce his words here in their entirety.

Dear Mr. Montague,

    I write in the first instance to inform you that a Native Boy has met his untimely Death here at Scrymgeour Station these two days past. I need hardly explain you that the presence of said Boy on

said Station leaves my Lot here in precariousness, *viz.*
the Native proclivity for violent Reprisal: to which
Problem I have recently Dedicated anew my Mind;
against which Problem I seek now to insure Myself.
It is perhaps my great Fortune then that the Death of
the Boy and Events concurrent therewith have perhaps
since furnished me with a Solution to said Problem. To
wit: heretofore I understood our Native Problem as one
founded upon competition for Pastoral Land, yet now
I wonder is it not one founded upon a Competition of a
more base Nature. Whereof I reflected upon the Nature
of the Intruder upon my Property, that he be no Man,
but a mere Boy, thereupon I perceived the Nature of
the Problem with Providential clarity.

I confess I strung the Boy up. My Purpose in so
doing, being to issue a Warning. But a Warning to
Whom? — not merely to other Men and Boys who
might rush forth and emulate this fanciful Pioneer,
but moreover to his Mother, that she might warn her
further Offspring of what Fate awaits them ere they
venture a Toe upon Scrymgeour Station. Yet, thought
I, that there should at all BE such a Mother serves
to disadvantage Me as regards the abundant Natives,
whose especial Advantage over me is I now see not
insignificant; namely, the Advantage
of REPRODUCTION.

Whereas they are a Multitude, as akin to the Hydra,
by which the Tribe has a capacity to replenish any

one lost Component, that the Whole may not suffer
irreparable Injury, I am but singular and finite and
thus vulnerable to their Hostility insofar as I am not
possessed of their Restorative Qualities. Consequently,
I contend, were I to eliminate or assauge the singularity
and finitude of Civilized Existence upon this Land,
so too would I claim Prowess to equal that which they
Possess. Thus I have concluded to relinquish the Title
to certain Allotments of my Property for transference
to whichsoever Man sees fit to raise his Family here at
Scrymgeour Station and when necessary to raise Arms
for the Betterment of our communal Venture. At your
earliest convenience, therefore, I ask that you reproduce
this Edict, effective immediately, that its Contents
appear in prominent Positions in the Broadsheets of
Rockhampton and Townsville. I intend to settle my
Account forthwith, on the Occasion of my next run to
Market, this 14th March 1889.

Yours, in humble Gratitude, I remain,

R. Scrymgeour.

Signed with the name he chose for himself. He must
have then followed or appended this letter with
another providing more specific instructions on the
settlement opportunities he hoped to offer. He must
have done so because those instructions appeared
in an advertisement published under his name on
April 1, 1889, in both the *Townsville Bulletin* and the

Rockhampton Morning Bulletin. That advertisement, comprising a summary of his intention to facilitate communal settlement, reveals more clearly the audacious particulars of Scrymgeour's vision for the Whangie. It limits to nine the number of available allotments and it specifies that only the first nine applicants deemed financially and physically suited to settlement will be allowed to stake a land claim. It specifies, too, that applicants may apply only in person and only if they bring at least one son fit enough to undertake farmwork, and then, identifying the prospective township by the name of 'Auchtermuchty Bend,' it identifies Mr Rowan A. Scrymgeour of Kirkintilloch, Dumbartonshire, as both the man behind the land offer and the township's honourable mayor-in-waiting.

I don't know who arrived first or who made the fastest start on the construction of a homestead. I don't know who settled in quickest or who curried favour with Scrymgeour ahead of all others. I don't know who received the most generous subdivision or who received the dregs of the land. The specifics of Scrymgeour's settlement are elusive. I can't say for sure that such and such a person built their house on this patch of earth, or that they brought in so many horses, or that they came from a particular place on the coast or a tiny town in Britain, or that they received this or that upbringing and supported so many children and hoped that they might here achieve x or y or z and so on. In a sense, the settlement of the Auchtermuchty Bend was a victim of its own success. The settlers carried it out with such enthusiasm and tenacity that the energies they expended invited the desolation of the place, much as a fire stoked to a rage will consume all its fuel in an instant and snuff itself out in a wisp of smoke. Today the township survives only through the foundations of the shanties that gash the landscape, and so its meagre history survives only through the broad strokes of its rapid rise and downfall. The first settlers appeared within two weeks of the publication of Scrymgeour's advertisement and established residency within a month of arrival. Twelve months after that, however, every one of those settlers would be dead and the settlement itself would be reduced to a smudge of black and grey across the parched white of the desert.

I wonder, but I cannot know, whether any of the men amongst those settlers considered the possibility that they were leading their wives and children to their doom. I wonder, but I cannot know, why those men who considered that possibility finally banished the thought and carried on with settlement. Were they fearless or were they foolish? Had they met with misfortune elsewhere and found themselves with no other prospects? I imagine them trudging westward from the cities, seedy, sweaty, exhausted, browbeaten, shambling towards the Whangie on the backs of drowsy horses and with emaciated wives and sons in tow. I imagine them throwing out torn and tattered canvasses under which women and children shelter themselves while the men negotiate deals with Scrymgeour. I imagine them unburdening their horses under the unwavering eyes of the girl who stands at the window, a silent sentry, now confined to the very house from which she had been so recently expelled.

After Abigail was released from the outhouse, after she saw the boy strung up on the hitching-post, after her father saw the blood between her legs and ordered her to clean herself in the river, a new set of orders was issued to her. She was to stop working the farm. She would now prepare basic meals and maintain the decorum of the house but she was to cease all manual labour. Her father would clean up the room she sullied and prepare it so she might properly rest. She would eat well and keep herself out of the sun. She would regain her pale skin and ease away the wiriness of her limbs. From time to time she would stand on the porch and peek at the cadaver still hanging high in the air, and as the days crept by she would mark its decay and decomposition. She would watch her father at work, she would await his return from Jericho when he rode there to deliver his letters, and she would come to know intimately the persistent paranoia that her mother must have felt when confined to a house so small in a place so expansive, so barren, so hopeless. Now, though, she stands at the window and observes the prospective settlers, one after another, making a bid for a patch of the Auchtermuchty Bend. The horses hunch under the harshness of the sun and only slowly escape the horizon. The first settlers, in sight of the Whangie, slip out of their saddles and trudge alongside their animals until the girl can see their faces. They are a man and a woman, both of them dustblown, as well as a boy somewhat older than she.

I imagine the man offers a perfunctory greeting, and asks where he might find this fellow Scrim-gee-ower. His question ends with an incorrect guess at a surname that mismatches script and sound. The girl replies with nothing but silence. The woman discerns something off in the distance, down the slope and at the far edge of the wheatfield, and with an outstretched finger she guides her husband's eyes to where Scrymgeour is hard at work. The man calls out, but too softly to be heard, so he takes his fingers to his mealy mouth and issues a whistle to make his presence known. Scrymgeour wheels around and, greeted by a friendly wave from the would-be settler and his wife, he starts uphill for the house. The man and woman await his arrival while the girl at the window eyes the boy, and then the girl watches the man observe and react to her father's approach. The unsettling of the posture when he notices Scrymgeour's limp. The slight flinch of the shoulder when the two men shake hands and the constriction of the arm, the effort not to flinch again, when Scrymgeour's words of greeting lisp out through the harelip.

Scrymgeour, I imagine, turns to his daughter and orders her to prepare damper while he shows their guests the Auchtermuchty Bend. The other man kicks at the dust, disappointed by the land he might freely take and yet unwilling to leave it to any one of the others whose horses are just now gathering in the east. The woman and her son select a space a few hundred feet from the Whangie, and there I watch them unfold the canvas that will serve as their shelter until they can build something more substantial. Then the first settlers of the next wave ride into view. While the girl waits for the damper dough to prove, she stands at the window and watches them come. One man, one woman, and two boys form one party, and one man, one woman, and four boys form the next. The formation repeats itself later that day and again in the days that follow as ever more settlers arrive at the Whangie. The men and women keep coming, and with them they keep bringing their boys.

On April 23, 1889, according to the *Rockhampton Morning Bulletin*, an expedition of eleven men set out for the port of Palmerston, now Darwin, on the far north coast of Australia. End to end, the overland journey was anticipated to take about five months to complete. Led by one Abraham Macwhirter, a Rockhampton sugarcane merchant apparently intent on making his name by some means other than sugar, the expedition was joined by only one man who had not requested to come along but had been commissioned to do so. His name was Samuel Eliot Culvahouse, and he too had grown sugarcane in Loganholme until, displaced by the floods of 1887, he decided to take up photography. The expedition was by all accounts successful. The party arrived at its destination on time and unhindered. Macwhirter reported that he had occasionally observed Aboriginal tribesmen *en route*, but he noted that they had maintained their distance and allowed his party to carry on without disturbance. The ferrotypes taken by Culvahouse are a pictorial echo of that report. The photographer recorded more than two hundred of the countless landscapes the expedition rode through on its way to Palmerston, each one presenting the vision of a continental interior as unsparing as it was unpeopled. Ten days out from the coast, but without having sent advance notice, Macwhirter's expedition showed up at the Whangie. Macwhirter requested of Scrymgeour some lodgings for the night and, according to the notes the visitor scribbled in his journal, Scrymgeour offered the barn and stable despite the scant space they afforded the travellers. But records of events that followed the end of the expedition reveal that Scrymgeour's interest was captured much less by its leader than by its documentarian.

I see Scrymgeour's settlement thriving with newcomers by the time the travellers reach it. I imagine the girl at first bewildered by the arrival of all these strangers and then, when bewilderment passes, I imagine she suffers increasing alarm. Her father told her nothing of his plans in the days after her release from the outhouse. He dispatched his edict to all the coastal broadsheets, then dislodged the dead boy from atop the hitching-post and patiently waited to receive a reply to his advertisement. The girl looked up at the post one day to see bones just barely sinewed together, but when she woke the next morning she found no trace of the remains. Her father explained nothing to her as settlers began to arrive after that. He left the house each morning before she had even awoken and he returned to the house each night long after she fell asleep. He spent his days now doing all the farmwork that would normally require the labours of the both of them and he spent his days this way without a word of complaint to her. I imagine the settlers dribbling in, a steady drip of newcomers, and I imagine the girl only slowly grasping the import of their arrivals. She has lost the battle. That is what their being here means. She might yet continue her sabotage, slitting the throats of the cattle or snapping the necks of the chickens, if not for the risk of intervention by any one of these new people. She might make more subtle manoeuvres, sneaking out under cover of darkness in order to wreak her havoc, if not for the risk of losing her life to a settler spooked by furtive footsteps in the night. Settlers sow new seeds and extend existing runnels to cultivate and irrigate the whole of the Auchtermuchty Bend. The foundations of new dwellings quickly become entrenched in the earth and after sunset each day, as darkness grips the Whangie, new sounds whirl above the river whose murmur once filled the night. Canvasses flap and flutter in the breeze. Horses stamp their hooves and slurp at the water provided to them. Human voices engage in chatter until a while after dusk, and then the snores of sleeping men drown out the shivers of the wives beside them. The mere presence of all these people leaves the girl immobilised. Each new arrival expands the settlement and tightens her father's grip on her.

In the several self-portraits he took during his journey north to Palmerston, Samuel Culvahouse appears as a severe and serious little man, gaunt of face with a pencil moustache and the cowlick fringe of a child. He peeps out of each frame with a furrowed brow and eyes so narrowed they have been reduced to slits. How exactly might Scrymgeour have set about approaching him? Culvahouse was responsible for the sole surviving ferrotype of the Whangie, published in the coastal broadsheets after the homestead burned. He staged that picture as dusk approached, and must have slipped away from his companions in order to do so, finding a vantage point far enough southeast to fill the frame with the homestead and the hitching-post and the cattle-pen fence. Did he peer too intently through the viewfinder to notice Scrymgeour out of the corner of his eye? Did the rush of the river drown out Scrymgeour's footsteps until the settler was already standing beside the other man? I imagine Scrymgeour bombarding his guest with questions to spark conversation. How great the complexities of a device such as the one the photographer carried? How hazardous the chemicals that develop the stock and what risk that the fumes might addle one's brain? Then, I imagine, he finds a way to lead the conversation elsewhere. Was it a satisfactory life to offer oneself to other men and follow them wherever they went? Was contentment easy to come by when one might spend all of one's days wandering the continent in the company of strangers? Was there no yearning, deep in one's heart, to settle down in a place where one might rest one's feet amongst friends and while away one's days in comfort? But of course I imagine Scrmygeour speaking like this to Culvahouse, appealing to him with visions of *better* and *more*, since that is exactly what he himself wanted and what he wanted to use the other man to get.

Scrymgeour had a dream, a vision, bigger than the petty settlers with whom he had just surrounded himself. In hindsight his dream looks like overreach, particularly since what would doom him was by this time done, but I see how the growth of his settlement could so inflame his desires as to blind him to the cataclysm already awaiting him. Scrymgeour's abiding suspicion, I think, was that the land that stretches out from Mackay to Palmerston, from the Great Artesian Basin to the Gulf of Carpentaria, was spiderwebbed across with a complex network of intersecting rivers. Somewhere along its northeastern journey from the Whangie to the coast above Mackay, the Auchtermuchty River intersected the Westmoreland. Then the Westmoreland, running northwest to southeast, possibly intersected the Gregory, which possibly intersected the Sleisbeck, which possibly intersected the Mary River, which ran to the Van Diemen Gulf and thus provided access to the thriving port at Palmerston. Scrymgeour wanted the Whangie to be an inland port at the other end. To make that happen he must have offered Culvahouse a deal. Find me a route to Palmerston and I'll give you your pick of my land, and, what's more, I'll even agree to build you your very own house on it. Find a route along those lines, connect the Auchtermuchty to the north coast of the continent, and you'd allow traders in the eastern ports to forgo the perils of reef and strait and follow a far easier route to markets in Batavia and Díli with the Auchtermuchty Bend as a major midway stopping point. You'd allow the fledgling settlement to blossom into a thriving community and a man with the equipment, the know-how, and the inclination could sit back and record its growth and esteem himself as chronicler of its evolution.

Of course the plan was too complex, too untested, and far too hazardous to ever become a reality. I can't imagine that Scrymgeour didn't already suspect as much, but I think he used Culvahouse to spread the word anyway to increase the odds of attracting commerce to his land. Culvahouse obliged without qualms. On October 2, 1889, a couple of weeks after the expedition reached its destination, the *Adelaide Advertiser* published a selection of his ferrotypes alongside an interview with the photographer himself. Dutifully reporting on a settler station newly founded on the banks of the Auchtermuchty, he announced that it now enabled northern merchants to reach the eastern ports in a way that avoided the coast. He declared that he intended to travel back to the station via the inland waterways and that, if all went well, he expected to arrive before Christmas. He looked forward to his return, he added, for the station was populated by many respectable family men whose sense of industry promised great things and whose generosity to strangers was without parallel.

For the record, the names of those men and their families were Ashberry, Bingham, Browne, Coughlan, Gilmour, Knox, Sadler, Wetherell, and Watkins. For the record, those names, along with the names of Scrymgeour and Culvahouse, are etched into the memorial plaque that now rests on the site where the hitching-post once stood and provides the only contemporary evidence that those slaughtered families ever existed.

One day, I imagine, after shanties have sprung up from horseloads of timber and gardens have sprouted from sacks full of seeds, an arrival from the west brings activity to a halt. The girl sits at the window and watches the new settlers from a distance when she notices a boy, almost a grown man, freeze where he stands to gaze into the sky. Then the two boys in his company freeze and a buzz flows through the settlers until, all over the property, everyone stops in their tracks, drops their tools and looks up towards the Auchtermuchty Escarpment. The girl follows their line of sight. Standing at the edge of the rocky rim are perhaps two dozen dark figures, half of them men and half of them children, gazing down in turn at the settlers beneath them. A chill creeps into the air, I imagine, despite the unbreakable heat of the day. It is the cold tension of an imminent storm wherein all you can do is wait for lightning to stammer across the sky. While the dark figures watch from above, the girl watches her father emerge from the wheatfield and turn to the settlers around him. He calls out to them in a demanding tone. He orders them not to shoot. He orders them not to antagonise the natives. He orders them to go back to their business and he promises that the strangers will momentarily depart. The settlers ignore him and remain where they are. He shouts, again, and insists that not a single shot be fired. Then his shout is followed by another. He swings around to peer up at the figures on the rocky rim and he raises a hand to his brow to battle the overhead glare. A young boy has stepped forward to shout something down to the settlers. A single word understood by none of them. It booms across the expansive land and the boy shouts it again, and again, so that it reverberates all around them and envelops them with sound.

Was it a name? Was it a threat? Was it perhaps a plea for peace? I would give almost anything to know what that boy shouted down to those people. I long to place on these pages one word, just one, with which to allow Scrymgeour's enemies to say something meaningful for themselves. For my part I struggle simply to find a word to name them with the respect they are owed, and more than that I struggle to find one that affords them some centrality. Natives. Tribesmen. Indigenous inhabitants of the Auchtermuchty Bend. None of the words available to me allow me to penetrate the barrier between them and myself. Whitewashing all their motives, all logic behind their actions, every word at my disposal insists on placing them in relation to Scrymgeour and the settlers who flocked to his land. Despite its awesome breadth and its flexibility, language here is too threadbare to encompass their experience, too impoverished to offer even some basic referent for what each tribesman was to himself, in himself, and to the loved ones in whose company private pleasures overshadowed tribal concerns. Having lost their language when they lost their lives, these men and their families have been lost to me and so I lose them in a thicket of abrasive and reductive nouns. This language, applied to them, advances an artifice that frustrates any understanding of who they actually were, and that's as true for those who use this language today as it was for the settlers enmeshed in it all those years ago. The tribesmen turned away from the rim of the escarpment and once more wandered out into the western deserts. Did they believe themselves to have been understood by the settlers standing beneath them? What could those settlers have even begun to understand when language as well as prejudice and circumstance armed them against empathy? Amongst the settlers, I imagine, there was a hope that those tribesmen saw before them the unstoppable growth of civilisation and were so overawed by it that they preferred to flee rather than force a confrontation. Yet, I imagine, the tension in the air did not disappear with the departure of the tribesmen and the likelihood of their return would have left many settlers anxious.

Shortly after that encounter, however, a shout from the riverside brings the settlers some relief with news that civilisation may yet reach them from the west as well as from the east. One of the settlers spots a small boat wending its way along the Auchtermuchty River. The girl sits on the porch and watches her father descend the slope to greet the boat at the bottom of the path. Samuel Culvahouse is burned raw and peeling when he steps onto land, steps out of the boat and into the mud. He brings with him two companions whose names I have been unable to establish, along with basic supplies of rice, flour, coffee, and tobacco, and a meticulous record of the route by which he found his way back to the Whangie. The summer is already blazing and a little less than two weeks will take the season to Christmas.

That night, I imagine, the girl prepares food for her father and his visitors as they sit and rest and talk together. Sometimes when I imagine this, this confirmation of a connection between the Whangie and the Gulf, I see the wrinkle of a smile slowly crawl across Scrymgeour's face. Often, though, I think I'm wrong to imagine a thing like that. Did he smile when he learned for certain that his land was the lynchpin between the eastern ports and Palmerston? Did he smile because he felt that his hold on this land had lasted, and had been strengthened, far beyond what he could have imagined when he set out to build the Whangie? I can't imagine that he was ever likely to betray any hint of his soul with a smile, but I also can't imagine that the return of Culvahouse brought him anything less than unbridled joy. When he wrote that letter to John Montague of Jericho, he twice identified his weaknesses as his own singularity and finitude. With settlers invited onto his land, he had already overcome the first weakness, and now, with Culvahouse promising a flourishing future for the settlement as a whole, he was decidedly on his way to overcoming the second.

Scrymgeour bows his head, I imagine, and allows himself a momentary smile. Then he raises his head again and seals the deal with Culvahouse.

The photographer says that he intends to visit Jericho in order to arrange the publication of his pictures in as many coastal broadsheets as will see fit to print them. Of course he adds that he intends to distribute them along with a new account of his travels concluding with his return to the Whangie. Scrymgeour once more guarantees him whichever allotment might strike his fancy and asks, in closing, if Culvahouse might do him the courtesy of running an errand when he conducts his business in town. There's a letter to be delivered to the postmaster-general, he says, and thence to be conveyed post-haste to Charleville. Culvahouse examines the envelope when Scrymgeour passes it to him. It is addressed, in Scrymgeour's spindly handwriting, to a recipient by the name of Officer Ernest Shadbolt.

Shadbolt arrives at the Whangie in two days although the journey should have taken him five. At dusk the girl sees him through the window and she sees his partner as well. Two men on horseback crest the horizon. She does not move to find her father. She stands at the window and watches as the other settlers notice the horsemen and hustle out of their makeshift homes to gather almost defensively at the edge of a road in the making. As the horses draw close to the Whangie and head towards the hitching-post, the girl recognises Shadbolt's face and then turns to take in the man beside him. The two men riding together offer a striking and somewhat fearsome sight. Shadbolt's companion is the colour of pitch. He sits high and straight in the saddle and must reach about six feet on foot. He has shockingly white but weary eyes and creases so deep at the corners of his mouth that they might have been gouged into his face. Taut skin around his cheeks and throat accentuates his jaw and his long, thin neck. He is shrouded in a heavy cloak, buttoned across a pigeon chest, and, like Shadbolt beside him, he wears the cap and insignia of the Queensland Colonial Police Force. He does not blink. He does not fail to notice the girl standing at the window. He does not look away from her when he climbs down from his horse and passes the reins to Shadbolt. The girl watches Shadbolt tether the horses to the post but then finds the black man still watching her when she looks at him again. The two men walk the gauntlet of settlers, the men and women and all their sons drawn to the freak show of a native in uniform, and then they stroll past the window and around the corner to reach the entrance to the homestead.

The girl hears her father caught by surprise. Ernest! he cries from somewhere down the slope. I didn't expect you for some time yet. His voice grows louder as he clambers uphill to the house.

I was already in Jericho when your letter arrived, says Shadbolt. I was already on my way to visit. There are some things I need to straighten out over there, y'see. Although, naturally, I'm happy to spend some time here with the young'n like you asked.

A momentary silence signals to the girl that this news has raised her father's suspicions. Well, then, he says as he draws closer to Shadbolt. As always, I must say I'm grateful for your assistance. Now. Come inside. Sit awhile. Take some refuge from the sun.

The Whangie trembles as her father steps onto the porch, followed by Shadbolt and then followed by the other man. No, no, says her father, not the tracker. Not in my house. You're welcome here, Ernest, but only you. The girl can imagine her father's squint as he sets his eyes on the black man. The tracker, he says, stays outside.

Shadbolt clears his throat. I apologise, he says, but he's here with me as my associate. And if he and me are here for a time while you're away in town, he'll have to come inside, no doubt. And as I'm sure you can see, my friend, he's much more than a simple tracker.

The silence at the front of the house suggests vexation beneath her father's composure. At last, though, the front door creaks open, and three sets of footsteps thunder inside.

The girl turns away from the window when the three men step into the homestead. Immediately Shadbolt doffs his cap while the black man does likewise with a nod. Nice to see you again, Shadbolt says to the girl before he turns to her father. May I introduce Mr Watlington? The black man remains unmoved while Shadbolt gestures in his direction. The name strikes the girl as absurd, I imagine, when worn by a tribesman like this, not to mention the buttoned-up collar, the greatcoat, the short-cropped hair, the buffed black boots. We received word, says Shadbolt, that you've had trouble keeping the local natives as settled as they should be. The girl watches for a reaction from the native in their company but Watlington reveals as little of himself as if he were chiselled from stone. We thought it worthwhile to assess the vulnerability of these parts, Shadbolt continues. Especially seeing as we've now been invited to stay a little longer for other purposes. My friend Watlington is here to help me survey the area as best we can and see if we can secure it, properly like, against any other troublemakers.

Charles Watlington, as he was christened, served as a Sub-Inspector in the Queensland Native Police Force established by First Corporal Frederick Walker in 1848. That year, Walker recruited more than a dozen troopers from various Queensland tribes to quell potential uprisings amongst indigenous peoples distressed by the inland expansion of settlement. The troopers were employed to persuade them to simply leave the settlers alone and swallow all complaints. In theory, they were to accomplish their aims through reason and through emotive appeals to ethnic and cultural kinship. In practice, they accomplished their aims more often through outrageous brutality. The tribesmen saw duplicity and treason in place of bonds that ran in the blood, while the troopers often used their authority to inflame intertribal conflicts. At bottom, the Native Policemen were outcasts. They had wedged themselves into furthering a war they could never win even when they emerged as victors

in its various battles. When I look at portraits of
Watlington now, several of which have survived the
years, I see a man devoured by a profound existential
dilemma. I do not know much about his history. I do
not know when he became a Native Policeman, nor
whether he did so of his own volition or whether he
was sought out and recruited by the powers that be.
He was certainly not one of the original troopers.
In portraits dated 1888 and 1889, he appears by my
estimate thirty years old. It's possible that he joined
the Native Police Force two or three years before
that and then rose through the ranks at speed. In
1888, Native Policemen killed some two hundred
Aboriginal adolescents, all boys, at a tribal gathering at Kaliduwarry on the Diamantina River, not
too far southwest of where the Whangie stood. The
slaughter came as a response to the murder of a white
cook, ostensibly committed by a party of tribesmen,
at a settler station newly established on a nearby site
called Durrie. That the response incurred no casual-
ties amongst the Native Policemen would have been
enough for any of those who took a leading role in the
attack to ascend the chain of command far quicker
than they might have otherwise done. It's possible
that Watlington followed that course. Whether he
actually did, I am not able to say. Whatever the case,
I find myself troubled when I look at his picture. I see
in him a viciousness born of private torments and the

jaded weariness of one enduring a hollowing out of the self.

I imagine that Scrymgeour despised Watlington on sight. I imagine that Scrymgeour looked at him and saw a barbarian who dressed up as a man while waiting for a chance to unleash his innermost urges. But then I worry that I have failed, now, to do justice to Scrymgeour, to consider whether he might have had a different and more sympathetic response to the arrival of the Native Policeman. From my vantage point over a century later, the two men seem to me far more alike than their superficial differences would suggest. Perhaps Scrymgeour recognised Watlington as a sort of accidental brother. Perhaps when he looked at him he saw, looking back, a version of the wretch he himself used to be.

In Scrymgeour's absence, Shadbolt and Watlington tended to the Whangie under the watch of Samuel Culvahouse. This I know for a fact. The Culvahouse ferrotypes, now digitally archived at the University of Queensland, are replete with pictures of Shadbolt and Watlington meandering around the Auchtermuchty Bend. Whether the visitors naturally aroused the interest of the photographer or whether Scrymgeour asked him to take an interest in their presence, the ferrotypes mark the progress of the officers in surveying the property. Watlington keeps to the distance, a black blot at the far edge of white dust, while Shadbolt remains close to the Whangie to keep an eye on the girl. Watlington follows the river for miles in either direction and at one point he even appears to have crossed it and climbed to the top of the Auchtermuchty Escarpment. His surveying notes, still accessible today, disclose approximate measurements of the height of the escarpment and the distances between buildings on the Bend, and, crucially, they even mark the location of the grave in which Scrymgeour buried his wife.

While Watlington surveys the site, I imagine, Shadbolt uses his time at the Whangie to find out as much as possible about the impetus behind Scrymgeour's little army of settlers. He hunts through the house for any hint of Scrymgeour's agenda and frustration rises within him when he finds a lock on the door to the forbidden room. The same frustration impels him to seek out the girl where she sits by herself on the porch and to approach her with a smile beneath that handlebar moustache. He takes a seat beside her and then, I imagine, he proposes a trade. He extends towards her a hand in which he holds a hardback volume. When her eyes alight on the volume, they widen and then they rise to meet his. Something happened here not long ago, he says. Something happened with one of the natives, and then your pa asked all these people to come here and put up these buildings. What I'd like to know is exactly what that thing was that happened. You'll tell me what you saw? There's a storybook for your troubles, he adds, and plenty more where this one came from. But the girl would have needed no book, no bribe, to reveal to Shadbolt everything she knew about what had happened to the boy who came to the Whangie that night, and so, I imagine, the end of her story left Shadbolt with only one unanswered question. If the body of that black-fella is gone, he says, I don't suppose you happened to see what your pa might've done with his bones? But, I imagine, the girl breaks her silence only to say that she saw nothing more. It's important, Shadbolt insists. Ask my mate Watlington just how important it is that he and me find where them bones are at. But the girl only chews at her bottom lip. She has nothing more she can give him.

Shadbolt increasingly interacts with other settlers as the passing weeks carry them into the Christmas season. This, too, I know for a fact. The names etched into the memorial plaque at the Auchtermuchty Bend were drawn from the notes he made during this visit to the Whangie. I imagine he approached the settlers with probing questions, or else with friendly conversation intended to answer the questions he kept to himself. What kinds of relationships had they formed with Scrymgeour? Did Scrymgeour lead this settlement in a political sense or did he only oversee its expansion? How irreproachable was his word? How readily would these people obey him? Would they follow him into war if he ordered them to do so? If they would, then why did he ask Shadbolt to watch over his daughter instead of asking the people around him? Did he want to be seen by them as someone with allies in positions of authority? Was the real purpose of Shadbolt's invitation here to aggrandise Scrymgeour and strike fear into anyone on the settlement who might rise against him? I imagine that Shadbolt received, at best, only partial answers to the questions he posed, although I imagine that he left the Whangie with no doubts about whether what was happening there would soon require another visit.

Scrymgeour returns after three weeks away and brings with him a thin wooden box. He offers Shadbolt and Watlington another night's lodgings and rest and then he rises at dawn to see them off to Jericho. When they are gone, he calls to the girl. When she approaches, he holds out the box. A belated Christmas gift, he says. She glances up at him, on guard, then steps forward to raise the lid and peer inside. What she sees is a fold of white fabric. She reaches into the box and lifts it out and lets it spill open and unfold to her feet. What she holds in her hands, she realises, is a long white gossamer dress. It is handwoven but shopworn, seamlessly stitched together, but a little threadbare and stained. I cannot say how Scrymgeour afforded it. Perhaps he traded a cow, or perhaps he requested a loan from a bank to be repaid using whatever funds he thought his daughter could bring him. The girl glances back up at her father as he holds the box forward for her to take another look inside. What she sees in there now looks like some strange accordion pieced together with fabric. She reaches in with one hand, holding the dress off the floor with the other, and takes out a small hourglass corset made of silk and whalebone. Her father sets the box aside. I'll help you put this on, he says. You and I are going to pose for a portrait. We both need to look our best.

This is how I imagine it happened. First he assesses her health as he would assess the health of a horse. He checks the condition of her teeth. He examines her eyes and her pallor. He runs a comb through her hair. He measures the girth of her arms and he lifts her off the ground to estimate her weight. Then he orders her to strip to her drawers. He wraps the corset around her and pulls on the laces to cinch her tight. He guides her into the dress and fastens it at the back. He leaves her inside the homestead while he goes in search of Culvahouse and then, when both men rumble the Whangie, he enters the forbidden room and leaves the photographer alone with the girl. The girl watches Culvahouse as he sets up his equipment. He moves silently and efficiently, tripod and plates and *camera obscura*, gradually fulfilling an arrangement made with

Scrymgeour long ago. Then the door to the forbidden room opens and Scrymgeour steps out in black trousers, a white-collared shirt, and a charcoal waistcoat. His hair is unkempt and his face unshaven, but his suit is sharp and immaculately clean. He converses easily with the photographer and dutifully arranges himself and his daughter in front of the waiting lens. He stands just behind the girl and drops his hand onto her shoulder the split second the shutter opens. When she flinches to avoid his grasp the portrait preserves her flinch for posterity. Four weeks later and more than one hundred years before it falls into my hands, reproductions of that ferrotype appear in the broadsheet newspapers of Rockhampton and Townsville. The man puts his daughter on show to the world as if selling a fine yearling filly at market.

N ow. It is no secret that I have taken certain liberties in the writing of these pages. I have followed the actual course of events as closely as I understand it and, where possible, I have drawn on historical records in order to do so. Beyond those records, however, and especially when moving from states of affairs to the states of mind of the people they involved, I have plunged into speculation and occasional invention. Why did the occupants of the Whangie behave the way they did? Why did they feel the need to push events in this or that direction? Because I can't know anything definite about what I want most to understand, I imagine and I imagine and I imagine some more. At this point, though, the broadsheet publication of the ferrotype portrait leads me to ask a more specific question. Why did Rowan Scrymgeour decide to sell his only daughter into a marital arrangement of which he himself would be the author? The reproductions of the portrait that appeared in print on February 11, 1890, were accompanied by a notice requesting offers of marriage from men no older than thirty years and stating that a price for the bride would be negotiable with Scrymgeour upon application. Why did he push forward with this sort of arrangement? I cannot say for certain. I can only guess. My belief is that he did it because he simply did not know anything different. What I have learned of his younger years is that he and his wife were wed, in England, after entering into an arrangement of an almost identical kind.

His wife. That poor woman. Her nervousness and despair. The suicide and her burial in the grave beside the river. How easy it can be, at first, to simply forget about all this. And yet that woman *was* someone, a human being with ideas and passions, with hopes and worries and pleasures and sufferings, and with no notion, no notion at all, that she was on her way to becoming those bones beneath the dust when, dressed up for a grand departure, her husband's hand in the small of her back guided her gently onboard the ship. By all accounts, the *Mary Pleasants* docked at Moreton Bay on August 8, 1857, and there Rowan Scrymgeour disembarked with his wife as if stepping into this world from some parallel universe. His name appears for the first time in the Colonial Secretary's Register of Immigrant Arrivals in what was then the colony of New South Wales. Although its appearance there may seem the innocuous result of standard immigration procedures, it is, in fact, remarkable. Two passenger logs were maintained for each ship that took migrants to the colonies of the British Empire. One was maintained by the Imperial Maritime Authority at the port of departure while the other was maintained by the relevant local authorities at the port of arrival. The name Rowan Scrymgeour appears only in the arrival log housed today in the Public Records Office of Queensland. The departure log, now housed in the British Empire and Commonwealth Museum in Temple Meads, Bristol, shows that a married couple by the name of Scrymgeour boarded the *Mary Pleasants* at Liverpool in 1857 but that the man recorded his first name as 'Aloysius'. With that name and the name Emmeline, the name of his wife, those bones in the riverside mud, I approached the General Register Office of England and Wales to track down their marriage certificate. That certificate was dated November 2, 1851, and revealed two details crucial to my reconstruction of the story of how those bones came to be where they lay. The first is that Emmeline's marriage to Scrymgeour had been officiated at and certified by the Reverend M.S. Chilton of Holy Trinity Church in Stroud, Gloucestershire. The second is that her full maiden name was Emmeline Annabel Tabitha Scrope, and her surname was one of wide repute in the locality where she and her husband were wed.

Taking the date of their marriage as a lead, I returned to Britain to follow their footsteps as far back as I could. In the Gloucestershire County Archives, I retrieved microfiche copies of the *Stroud Journal* for seven days on either side of November 2, 1851. I hoped that a report or a notice of the marriage would provide the names of family members through whom I might trace the lives of these people. Since the marriage took place on a Sunday, it was not reported immediately because no newspapers were printed on that day or the next. On Tuesday, November 4, however, a notice appeared not merely amidst or alongside other notices but above them all, just under the masthead, in a black frame as wide as the three central columns of text. It announced 'the joining together in Holy Matrimony of his Beloved Daughter, Emmeline, and Honourable Acquaintance, Aloysius Scrymgeour', and wished the couple 'all the Blessings of Providence in their Voyages Abroad', and it was attributed to a man whose name, in large print, far overshadowed the names of husband and wife: 'the Hon. George Julius Poulett Scrope, MP, JP, Representative of the People of Stroud'.

Stroud is a small town west of England's Cotswold Hills, set down in a depression where five long valleys converge, and, being only five miles south of the city of Gloucester, it gives its name to the parliamentary constituency that covers most of southwestern

Gloucestershire. George Scrope had been elected as the Member for Stroud in a by-election in 1833 and ultimately held his seat until he retired in 1867. In 1851, however, his re-election at the poll scheduled for the following year was anything but guaranteed. The ruling Whig and Liberal coalition had recently found a new base of support in the urban centres of Britain while voters in more rural areas had swung towards the Conservatives. As a Liberal establish-mentarian representing an increasingly Conservative electorate, Scrope was already facing an uphill strug-gle to retain his seat and his woes were only worsened by other aspects of his character. Twenty years of parliamentary service had made him a somewhat stale presence, his reputation had been damaged by revelations that a son long ago born to a mistress had received parliamentary assistance in securing an Eton education, and his only legitimate child, Emmeline, remained unmarried at age nineteen when she should have been tending to children of her own. To better appeal to the Conservative worldview and to burnish his credentials as a family man, Scrope embarked on a reinvention and reinvigoration of his public persona. A timely wedding, publicly announced, would perhaps generate a surge of goodwill sufficient to overshadow his public misfortunes and to shore up the stature of his venerable family name.

There was just one problem with this idea. Scrope

possessed a vast private fortune, the future of which he needed to secure. Having entertained an abiding fascination with geology and mineralogy since his undergraduate studies in Cambridge, Scrope had spent several years in Naples and Sicily to conduct fieldwork on Vesuvius and Etna before returning to Britain to invest in tin and coal mining enterprises in Cornwall and southern Wales. By 1851, with his investments generating an annual income more than seven times greater than his parliamentary salary, he seems to me to have held an interest in finding an heir whom he could keep firmly under his thumb. Here, again, I speculate based on what I know of the man's own youth. Born as George Julius Poulett Thomson in 1797, he married Emma Phipps Scrope in 1821 and thereafter adopted his wife's surname rather than allowing her to adopt his. The reason he adopted her name was that their marriage had been arranged and authored by her father, William Scrope, who had established himself as his son-in-law's patron and even offered him residency at Castle Combe, Wiltshire, which his family had owned since the fourteenth century. George Scrope was therefore the beneficiary of the respect commanded by his wife's family name, and so her family was able to exert a certain leverage over him. What he wanted in turn, I think, was to allow a young man to similarly benefit from inheriting the name from him and, in the process, to acquire for himself an underling who would be forever in his debt.

Because his accounts were comprehensively documented during his years in Westminster, his expenditures now speak of the urgency of his search for a son-in-law. I imagine his daughter both speechless and anxious as his search quickly gathers momentum, in much the same way as Abigail was when Scrymgeour surrounded himself with those settlers. I imagine her bewildered by his newly frenetic behaviour and unsettled, too, by the secrecy of his dealings. In regional newspapers all over the country, he places advertisements requesting the attention of eligible bachelors. In at least one advertisement in the *Hull Packet*, and I presume in several other publications that I have been unable to locate, he mentions up-front that he seeks an enterprising young man not only willing to wed his daughter but also to transact family business abroad and throughout the colonies. Gold was discovered in New South Wales in the first week of 1851. My guess is that Scrope received word of the discovery in March or April and decided, then and there, that any future son-in-law must be willing to voyage to Australia to establish a mine in the family name. He engaged in correspondence with at least a dozen potential suitors and then, between April 12 and August 21, he met face-to-face with candidates to assess their desirability. In his financial ledgers, he itemised train journeys to and from Bournemouth, Bath, Newquay, Norwich,

Hull, and Coventry under the euphemism INHERIT-
ANCE INQUIRIES. Presumably he found something
unsatisfactory about the young men he met in those
places, since he went on to take a journey to Glasgow
on Wednesday, September 3, after which his inquiries appear to have ceased. In Glasgow, then, he found,
or thought he found, just the sort of man he had been
searching for.

When Scrymgeour called for settlers to join him
at the Auchtermuchty Bend, he identified himself as hailing from the town of Kirkintilloch,
Dumbartonshire, eight miles northeast of central
Glasgow. I can find no reason to believe that he came
from anywhere else. Although the ancestral lands of
his clan lie in the vicinity of Cupar, his surname is
common in the Scottish midlands and, at the base
of Auchineden Hill, some thirteen miles west of
Kirkintilloch, a cluster of enormous boulders stands
cleaved apart by a three-foot-wide chasm which,
amongst locals, is known as the Whangie. Those
details are enough to satisfy me that Scrymgeour
did indeed originate from Kirkintilloch, and that his
being there was what attracted the interest of the man
who would become his father-in-law. Scrope was a
typically patrician Victorian gentleman, slender and
straightbacked and sporting a beard and moustache
cultivated with care. I imagine he was thrilled to enter
correspondence with a lowly Scottish peasant, and

I imagine he was thrilled again to find that peasant an outcast even amongst his own worthless people. A limp, a harelip, and polydactyl appendages. Signs of degeneracy, idiocy, and shame. A conversation with Scrymgeour would have been enough to disabuse Scrope of any prejudices against the intelligence of the luckless Glaswegian, but the lucklessness itself would have been enough to satisfy him that Scrymgeour would do well to marry Emmeline. He needed a young man devoid of real ambition but desperate to claw his way out of a poor station in life. He needed someone who yearned to escape from what he had been born into and who would therefore give himself up to anyone who offered the slightest helping hand.

I wish I could picture Emmeline Scrope on the day of her marriage to her husband, but her bones are all I can see in my mind because none of her portraits have survived the years. Who knows what she felt as she walked down the aisle, as her father prepared to give her away to the wretch awaiting her at the altar, or what any given emotion might have looked like when it manifested on her face? I wish I could picture Scrymgeour as well, but even he eludes me because, on that day, the only portrait of him that survives was still thirty years away from being taken. The only face I can picture, then, is the face of the father of the bride. With a smile broad and beaming, he makes no effort to hide or suppress a happiness that approaches bliss. He had good reason for that happiness. He was right to suspect that the marriage of his daughter would yield him the goodwill and success he sought so desperately at that time. Although the Whigs and Liberals lost the election of 1852, Scrope managed to retain his seat and would hold it for more than a decade to come. Within a few years of the wedding, however, the old man incurred a misfortune that would lead him to see his earlier celebrations as disastrously premature.

First he encouraged Scrymgeour to follow in his footsteps and adopt the name of his father-in-law. Then, over the course of five years, he set about recasting the young man as a facsimile of himself. He tested him at the reins of his mining enterprises and he dispatched him to Wales and Cornwall to supervise the activities there. He encouraged him to research mining opportunities elsewhere in the British Empire, and he instructed him to redouble his efforts following reports of the gold rush in Victoria in the early 1850s. He educated him in what were then the modern sciences, having been appointed a Fellow of the Royal Society for his contributions to geology in 1826, and in doing so he awakened in Scrymgeour a hunger to observe, to analyse, to understand, and to report on the workings of the natural world. What quiet hours must they have spent in the dank and mouldy chambers of a castle that Scrymgeour in his previous life could not have even hoped to set eyes on? What nights must they have shared in mumbled elocution lessons, unpicking the Scotsman's unacceptable accent one syllable at a time? I can smell the brandy on the old man's breath as Scrymgeour leans in close to listen. I can hear the scratch of a quill on parchment when the old man corrects the economics questionnaire he has ordered his pupil to complete. I can only guess how often the real Scrymgeour surfaced while suffering the designs of the overbearing Scrope. How often did he think back to his boyhood as a peasant and linger over his memories of his gaunt, famished parents, swept away by the swells of history, with whom he must have been ordered to sever all ties and all contact? How often did he lie with his wife and unintentionally reveal, by a lapse in forced conversation, that he saw her as nothing but an instrument for material gain and that in his heart he assigned her no more human dignity than he would assign the shoes on his feet? However often the mask of genteel manners might have slipped, it did not slip often enough for Scrope to suspect that Scrymgeour was anything other than the agreeable acquaintance he appeared to be. Between late 1851 and early 1857, between Scrymgeour's marriage to Emmeline and their emigration to Moreton Bay, the two men worked together so closely and so frequently that the elder man seems to have been convinced that Scrymgeour was ably and honourably the very protégé he hoped to find. That is to say that

Scrymgeour convinced him of his virtues by blinding him to his true intentions. Scrymgeour was no protégé. Scrymgeour was a parasite.

In mid-1856, Scrope wrote a cheque for £15 made payable to one A.M. Gillingham of Botany Bay in return for what he itemised as SURVEYING SERVICES. Since it would not have been prudent to pay so large a sum to a total stranger, I assume he and Gillingham corresponded before he dispatched Scrymgeour to New South Wales to chase up the opportunities presented by the surveyor. In April of the following year, Scrope wrote a second cheque for the purchase of two tickets aboard the *Mary Pleasants*, leaving Liverpool for Moreton Bay, at a rate of about £35 per person. In May, as Scrymgeour and his wife prepared to board the ship, Scrope wrote three more cheques, each one for the sum of £50, and gave them to Scrymgeour so that he might meet what were itemised as LAND PURCHASE & LIVING EXPENSES. Totalling more than five times the annual earnings of the average Englishman, and somewhere between twelve and thirteen times those of the average Scotsman, it is difficult to overstate the scale of the funds that Scrope provided to Scrymgeour. To give Scrope the benefit of the doubt, I imagine him writing those cheques for Scrymgeour with some glimmer of charity in his heart along with a great swell of pride. I imagine him satisfied that he had etched the best of his own talents into the *tabula rasa* of the young man and that, at the same time, he had afforded Scrymgeour a quality of life he could never have attained on his own. Yet I also imagine Scrope overcome by a rush of anxiety, a fear that perhaps his investment in Scrymgeour will prove to have been a terrible mistake, and then, in the weeks and months after the *Mary Pleasants* has set sail for distant lands, I imagine the growth of that anxiety as the passage of time assaults him with his son-in-law's inexplicable silence.

Scrope's meticulous financial records offer a sketch of the story. In August 1857, he marked down a payment for international postage to Australia. Scrymgeour and his wife would have been under strict instructions to send immediate word of their arrival at every port on their voyage. If Scrope waited until August to write to them in Australia, he probably received letters from Lagos, Port Elizabeth, and Mauritius in early June and throughout July before the communications came to a halt and the silence settled in. He recorded more postage payments in early and late November and then three times in December. Signs of a rising panic. Given the time and the cost required for deliveries to Australia, the most logical thing for Scrope to do would have been to save up everything he wanted to say and write it all out at once. He didn't. He wrote, and he wrote, and he wrote again. He wrote in bursts as if to encourage a response that never came. I imagine anxiety souring into anger. I imagine the powerlessness he must have felt in the depths of all that silence and I imagine the impossibility of acknowledging, slowly, that he had fallen victim to a fraud. For six years he had invested himself in the future of a man he embraced as a business associate, a friend, a son, and an heir, and he had gambled a vast amount of time and money in support of his investment. He had acted as adviser, as tutor, as father, and sometimes as disciplinarian, and he had offered Scrymgeour his trust, his wealth, his name, his reputation, his very livelihood, not to mention his daughter and his bloodline. It could not have been easy for him to acknowledge, when faced with Scrymgeour's continued silence, that everything he had given had been lost to him, stolen from him, as soon as his son-in-law and his daughter stepped aboard that ship. It could not have been easy for him to admit that all of it, all six years spent in company with that man, had brought him face-to-face with a deception far greater and more sophisticated than any he ever thought possible, a deception sustained with formidable care and endurance, from at least the moment Scrymgeour clambered out of that train in Glasgow and even perhaps from the moment he read the old man's plea for a son-in-law and decided he would answer.

When I think of the duration and depth of the charade, when I sit down and try to fathom the sort of willpower it must take to graciously accept years of courtship and marriage and business arrangements and the cultivation of an ultimately unwanted connection, I find myself awestruck, again, by the unparalleled patience of Rowan Scrymgeour. If only I could isolate and convey the power of every element in the brew of emotions he must have kept bottled up all that time. The hunger for the fortune he envisioned in his future. The contempt for the patronising custodianship of his father-in-law. The resentment at the circumstances into which he had been born and the raging ambition, the very ambition Scrope overlooked, that fuelled him and allowed him to persevere and endure the hardships he encountered. I imagine the excitement that sparked inside him when he shucked off the false name of Aloysius Scrope and gave his real surname to the record keepers at his port of departure. I imagine the relief that must have washed over him when he boarded the *Mary Pleasants* and felt the ship unmoor from the dock and pitch and roll out to sea. I watch him stand tall on the open deck as a fierce wind at his back sweeps him on towards a new and more liberated life. He creaks across the planks with the seabreeze setting his hair atumble, his greatcoat writhing all around him, and as he looks back to land from the stern of the migrant ship he watches his old country recede to a thin line resting atop the waves. He stalks the decks as the ship picks up supplies at ports along the coast of Africa, and at night he descends into the hold, the restless ocean lapping at the wooden bulk, to indulge in the first spell of leisure he has ever encountered and to spend time contemplating the sort of man he might become. That is perhaps why it is so difficult for me to articulate Rowan Scrymgeour. He made himself into something more than just a single man, he evolved himself into many men inside a single body, and he defined himself so that only he could ever say who he really was. I imagine him now disembarking in Queensland with the sweltering sun overhead, and I imagine the strange but refreshing sound of his new name the first time he lets it tumble from his lips. He steps off the deck of the ship to approach the authorities at his port of arrival, and he makes himself known to them as the man he is to me. He calls himself Rowan Scrymgeour and I cannot say exactly why. Perhaps he simply felt a fondness for the rowan tree.

I imagine him grasping his wife by the hand and leading her into town through the crowd. He feels a boundless freedom as they vanish amidst those innumerable faces, as well as a creeping panic when he senses his freedom endangered the longer he lingers at Moreton Bay. He secures lodgings and a meal for the night and he watches his wife write a note to her father. He takes it from her the following morning with the promise that he will arrange for its postage and then, stepping outside by himself, he tears it to shreds and throws it away. He cashes the three cheques and claims his funds and spends them quickly in the following days. He purchases a horse and a licence for the first leg of a droving run, and he leases a tiny house far up north in Rockhampton. It could not have taken his wife very long to object that what he was doing was not at all what her father had asked of him. It likely took her a little longer to realise that her husband had severed contact with home and that she, like her father, had been monumentally deceived. I imagine his nonchalance when she summons the courage to confront him, his indifferent shrug of the shoulders and apathetic admission of guilt, and I imagine he leaves her at home to retreat from the new world around her, to slowly descend into herself, as he plans and plots the future they will share in Australia.

Plans aside, this is how it will be. Thirty-odd years on a droving run. Months of separation and solitude at a stretch. The massacre at Hornet Bank just weeks after their arrival. The dispersals offering ready-made alliances with men of reputation. The gazetting of the inhospitable deserts and the piecemeal construction of the Whangie. Parenthood, a son and daughter, and then, when the homestead is ready to be lived in, the westward migration that will drive Emmeline to her death. I imagine Scrymgeour imagines a quiet life when he first secures his land, perhaps even a life devoted mainly to study, supported by his droving cattle every few months while his wife stays at home to tend to the farm and the children. Now, though, with her bones in the ground so many decades after he cut her off from her father, I imagine him envisioning a future of a very different sort. The settlers assemble new dwellings across the Auchtermuchty Bend. The girl clenches up in the corset and the dress he bought for her. The ferrotype portrait appears in the broadsheets alongside the advertisement appealing for suitors. I imagine he imagines he will safeguard himself against any young man who would do to him what he knows he did to his own father-in-law. I imagine he imagines he can exert more control over a suitor than anyone could ever possibly have exerted over him.

But the girl, *his* girl, is a feisty little insurrectionist. She would deny him his self-sufficiency with as much insistence as her grandfather before her. I imagine he imagines he must lock her in her place. He distributes the ferrotype portrait to the young bachelors of Rockhampton and Townsville and many small towns between the two cities. Since the recent skirmishes in Africa mean that there may not be too many young men to be found on the coast in the months ahead, he appeals to them while he knows he is able. He wants the right young man to stumble across his advertisement. He wants the right young man to find him and come to his door. What he does not know is that, at this very instant, he is already being sought out by a young man of his own blood and he has just announced his whereabouts to whoever might want to find him.

O n blazing days, in this part of the country, there's nothing to do but sit and sweat it out. Humidity hits its high before dawn, but storm clouds will take all day to seep across the sky and the downpour won't begin until the day begins to darken. Best find somewhere to still yourself and try not to move a muscle. Ignore the sweat pooling in your armpits and your groin and ignore the insects that cling for life to your slickening skin. React to those small tortures and you'll find yourself awash in still more perspiration. React too often and you'll grow lightheaded, perhaps dehydrated, and it's only a small step from there to a faint. There's nothing to do but sit and sweat it out. Suffer the weight of the water in the air and watch it drown all possible movement as if thrusting the whole world into slow motion.

Scrymgeour, I imagine, spends the morning immersed in study inside the forbidden room. The girl lies languid on the porch where she listens to the whine and whir of the flies. Both of them are oblivious to the five men on horseback until the horses are almost upon them. The moisture that thickens the air muffles the clopping of hooves. Only when the girl hears a distant cough and a sigh does she turn her head to find the men approaching the Whangie. She holds fast to the side of the homestead and takes to her feet. All five men are in uniform. She recognises two of them. I have not been able to find records that name the other three. The girl slips into the house, her skin already ashine with sweat, and raps her knuckles against the door to the forbidden room. After a moment the door swings open and Scrymgeour ambles out. Yes? He frowns at the girl, expecting a reply, but quickly turns to the window when the sounds of the oncoming party spill through it. He peers out the window, trying to discern the faces of the horsemen, then he moves to the front door and, as he exits, barks an order at the girl behind him.

Do not move from here, he says.

With that curt command, I imagine, Rowan Scrymgeour enters his final twenty-four hours of life. The house in which he now stands will burn to the ground this time the next day. The sparks that will ignite the flames are flying towards him as he walks through the door, and those five men on horseback will be the first to strike the tinder. I worry that this seems improbable when thrown so bluntly onto the page. I worry that it might seem too far-fetched to be true and that, in some sense, I have therefore failed the men and the girl who long ago experienced the events I'm preparing to depict. I worry that by wedging their lives into the shape of a story, by compressing and excising the tedium that consumed the bulk of their days, I have stripped them down to inhuman cogs churning inside a narrative machine, or else I have recast them as puppets prancing from one staged vignette to the next. Even so, I see no way to detail what I know happened to them except as directly as I am able. The available police records show that five men on horseback visited Scrymgeour late in the morning of the day before his settlement was razed. But since those records do not detail the minutiae of the visit, I can only imagine how those men fuelled the flare that made a flashpoint of the Whangie.

The girl positions herself at the window from where she watches the scene outside. Her father limps through the sweltering heat to await the horsemen at the hitching-post. Shadbolt and Watlington are the first to dismount. They pass the reins of their horses to two of their companions and, as the horses are tethered to the hitching-post and their third companion sets off to fetch water, the two of them saunter over to where Scrymgeour stands. Shadbolt is a mess of sweat. He removes his hat and smooths his hair back over his glistening pate. He extends his hand to Scrymgeour but finds Scrymgeour unwilling to shake it. Scrymgeour, ignoring Shadbolt, glowers at Watlington beside him. Watlington remains expressionless while his eyes rove over the property. When he finds Scrymgeour observing him with almost obsessive attention, he stares back at the settler with no other movement.

So, says Scrymgeour, an unbidden arrival.

But, says Shadbolt, I hope a not unwelcome one.

So do I. But of course it depends on the nature of the business that brings you here. Scrymgeour indicates the nearby strangers with a quick upward jerk of his chin. You ride all the way out here without announcing your arrival and you drag these companions along with you and the way I see it is you're fixing to get the jump on me for something untoward.

Care to name what that might be? Shadbolt smiles at Scrymgeour. No need to lose your calm. Nobody here can get the jump on you unless you've got something to hide. Right?

Scrymgeour furrows his brow. Spit it out. What's your business here?

At that moment, I imagine, the girl finds Watlington's eyes returning to her. He gazes hard up into the window just as he did the first time he came. A moment passes, though, and the gaze softens and just barely shifts. Watlington looks up through the window but he is not looking at the girl standing by it. Something behind her has captured his attention. She turns, just slightly, to look, and she sees then that her father has ventured outside without closing and locking the door to the forbidden room. By the time she turns back to Watlington, he is already on the move. Scrymgeour marks his movements until Shadbolt seizes Scrymgeour's attention. See here, says Shadbolt as he pulls a sheaf of papers from a satchel strapped across his torso. Scrymgeour takes the papers from Shadbolt and scans the first page and then flips through the rest. Names, he says. A list of names. And what am I to do with this? He returns his scrutiny to Watlington as the Native Policeman heads for the house.

A roll, not a list, says Shadbolt. Haven't you heard the news?

Scrymgeour arches an eyebrow. News is late to reach us here.

Shadbolt taps at the papers Scrymgeour holds in his hands. Articles of conscription, he says. Don't play the fool, Rowan. You mightn't have heard the news but you must've heard the rumours. We're trying to bolster our numbers.

In an instant Scrymgeour releases the Native Policeman from his sights and turns to fix his deep-sunk eyes firmly on his friend.

We need a roll of names, says Shadbolt, and we're empowered to take it. The Crown wants to know who's eligible and who's not, and whether or not the eligible are fit to take up arms when asked.

I imagine Scrymgeour squints at Shadbolt and sees, in place of an old associate, the uniformed lackey of a faceless power who has relinquished all his old supportive ties. Through his squint, I imagine, Scrymgeour searches for some manifestation of whatever it is inside the man that has driven him to offer himself to an unappeasable overlord. Whatever it is lies beyond Scrymgeour's view and beyond his comprehension, but, I imagine, he cannot stop himself from searching for it anyway. Shadbolt only sighs.

While Scrymgeour glares at Shadbolt in silence, Watlington gently quivers the Whangie. The Native Policeman steps onto the porch and quietly, almost inconspicuously, eases into the house. The girl turns to find him stepping in through the door.

There's been trouble in Burma and Egypt, Shadbolt says outside. Beads of sweat slip down his face and, beneath his heavy uniform, his undergarments gather between folds of flesh and grow wet. There's been a little trouble in Somaliland too, and in West Africa and suchlike. Skirmishes all round. Not that the Crown wants to send anyone out there from here anytime soon, you understand. It's just that the higher-ups want to know who might be called to service if they happen to see the need to issue the call someday.

Watlington steadily advances on the girl in the

house but still he looks through her and past her instead of looking directly at her. The door to the room just behind her remains the focus of his attention.

The trouble is, says Shadbolt, we can't have you keeping so many young men out here when they might be necessary to the Crown in time of war. You can keep them here, of course, but we need to know who we can call, and where to call them, if the need ever arises.

These men, Scrymgeour growls, are already at war. We are fighting a war out here.

Watlington pauses beside the girl. He glances through the window at the outside scene. A crowd of settlers has begun to gather around Shadbolt and the other three officers. Scrymgeour still holds the papers in his hands and with one, two, three quick jerks he shreds the thin sheaf and lets the torn pages fall and scatter at his feet. Watlington turns away from the window and treads gently towards the forbidden room. The girl turns to follow him and watches him from behind.

This is a very petty dispute, says Shadbolt.

You've no right to lay claim to these men, says Scrymgeour. They are their own masters and they serve no other.

The Crown has every right to them. The Crown is the Crown and we are its subjects.

The Crown claims sovereignty over this land but it cannot exert sovereignty over the natives west of here.

I am facilitating the extension of its sovereignty and these men are helping me in my efforts. We serve the Crown where we are.

Well, says Shadbolt, the Crown may one day need them to serve elsewhere.

Watlington lingers at the door to the forbidden room and surveys the scene before him. The girl, peering around him, can see only a little of what he must be able to see. The desk bestrewn with open notebooks, empty inkwells, broken quills. The desk and all its chaos, its decanters of preservative fluid, its strips of shredded muslin and its clumps of cotton wadding and other scraps of whatever Scrymgeour used to handle his specimens, and all this alongside a doughy damper left half-eaten, chunks of marl chiselled out of the ground, candles shrunk to waxen nubs, and a clamour of similar sights and samples that blanket the desk in a mess of dusty white.

Mark my words, says Scrymgeour. If the Crown believes that its claim to this land amounts to a claim on the men who live here, the Crown will fire the opening shot in a war to be waged on its western front.

Watlington now turns away from the door, away from the room, and peers again through the window. The girl follows his lead. Shadbolt, outside, looks aghast. You wouldn't dare, he mutters. You wouldn't *dare*. You'd have to be insane.

Scrymgeour thrusts a finger at Shadbolt's chest.

I would dare, he says. I would dare because I know that the Crown will not attack its own people. The Crown depends on those people, these people, to tame the natives of this continent. It would not want others elsewhere on the frontier to fall under the impression that such people are expendable.

Watlington silently passes the girl as he moves back to the front door of the Whangie.

Shadbolt lowers his voice. You'll get yourselves killed, he says to Scrymgeour. You will have these people wiped out if you provoke the Crown. He looks around, incredulous, at the settlers who have gathered at the edge of the Whangie. You know me, he says to the men in the crowd. I spoke to you. I took your names. All I need now, y'see, is for you to sign the roll. I'm not asking you to fight. I'm just asking you to confirm that you are who you say you are. Perhaps he expects at least one of the settlers to speak out as the voice of reason and to try to persuade Scrymgeour to acknowledge the authority of a representative of the Crown. If he expects any such thing, his expectations must be quick to die. The settlers stand by, sweating in silence, while Scrymgeour catches Shadbolt's eye with all the authority that anyone could possibly muster in this community. Rowan, says Shadbolt. Be wise.

Scrymgeour squints again at his former ally. You, he says softly. Be gone.

The men climb onto their horses and saunter off through the wary crowd. I imagine the bitterness on Shadbolt's tongue as he dwells on the weary hours he wasted on the sweaty slog from Jericho and I imagine Watlington riding beside him in silent contemplation. The horsemen strike out for the darkening clouds in the east. Spidery scrub pricks the heels of their animals. The crowd disperses, defeated by the humid heat, when the horses and their riders finally vanish from view.

I imagine Scrymgeour containing his rage as he slumps back into his homestead and rocks it into motion. I imagine his frown at the girl when he sees her at the entrance to the forbidden room, but I imagine he is too burdened by his concerns with Shadbolt to make much of his failure to lock the door behind him. He slouches past his daughter and into the open room, and then looks over his shoulder at her as if beckoning her to follow. While she hovers there at the threshold he runs his fingers along the edge of the desk, and then he plods around the desk and drops down into the chair behind it. He sits at the desk and watches her at the door, and he waits for her to recognise what lies in front of them both. I imagine a change coming over the girl, a slow and subtle alteration in the composure of her face, as she surveys the white wreckage scattered across the desk and realises that not all of it is waste. Did Watlington see clearly what she had at first overlooked? Amidst the mess of cotton and damper and marl and wax lies the missing skeleton. The bones of the dead boy are here. Every toe and finger joint, every leg and arm bone, and all the vertebrae and ribs and the skull as well have been laid atop the desk and reassembled. The left shin has been laterally split where the iron jaws bit into it. Branching fractures in the right cheekbone are the footprints of a kick to the face. Various instruments have gathered around the wreckage. A magnifying glass and a pair of tweezers. A ruler and calipers and pages of notes. No rotting flesh, the bones wiped clean, but enough remnants of a rancid smell to still attract the flies. Her father's deepsunk eyes hover above the bones and burn directly into the widening eyes of the girl. He rises from where he sits and grabs the back of the chair with one hand, and then he drags it to the far side of the desk and gestures for the girl to take it. Sit, he says, and sweat it out. She collapses into the chair.

The bones stretch out before her. She bows her head to avoid the sight while her father leans back against a wall and calmly, gently, closes his eyes.

They sweat it out together. Neither of them says a word but neither one hears silence. Flies and a dragonfly flit into the room to play at the gaps in the floorboards and walls. The hours skulk past at a sluggish pace as the day drags itself towards dusk. There is a whiff of ozone in the air when the girl, raising her head at last, finds her father with his eyes on her. At first, I imagine, her whole body goes stiff as she meets his fixed look and forces herself not to falter. Then, I imagine, she notices her father's eyes flicker from her face to her stomach and there, on her stomach, she feels a light weight, a delicate pressure, as something disturbs the fabric of her dress. Without moving her head she forces a downturn of the eyes and just glimpses, at the edge of her vision, the hornet striped in black and gold and humming its wings so fast it snarls. She does not need to see the size of the thorax and barb. They don't matter. Hornets don't just sting, they bite, they bite and they keep biting until their victims are covered over with welts. The girl looks up at her father. The house sways under his step. He leans forward to lift a jar from the desk and then, taking a piece of paper in hand, he stands in front of the girl and carefully leans towards her. The hornet snarls again with the humming of those wings and, perhaps sensing the presence of the man, it wanders here and there with jagged steps across the fabric. Suddenly Scrymgeour thrusts the jar against his daughter's stomach and forces the hornet to take flight and rush into the closed end of the glass. Then he just barely lifts the jar off her dress and slips the paper over the open end to trap the hornet inside. The girl releases a tense breath when her father carries the hornet away.

When he sets the jar on the desk the hornet lashes out, tinkling itself against the glass and then alighting on the paper and sharpening its wings while twitching around in circles. Scrymgeour reaches for a pile of supplies pushed up against the edge of the desk and plucks out the two-thirds melted stump of a candle and a worn and flimsy book of matches. He strikes a match, tosses the matchbook aside, and lights the tiny candle which he holds in one hand. He drops the match to the floor and then reaches for the jar, sliding the paper out from under it as he drags it to the edge of the desk. At this renewed movement the hornet kicks itself as high as possible into the air, protesting against the ceiling of its glass prison, and when it does so Scrymgeour lifts the lip of the jar off the edge of the desk to place the burning candle inside. He slides the jar, the candle, and the hornet together back towards the centre of the desk, back towards the bones, and then he leaves them sitting there. The insects encased in tubes around him, or those he has fixed into place with pins jabbed through their fragile bodies, are evidence of his having often done what he is doing now. He stands above the glass jar and with his daughter beside him he watches the hornet overtaken by death. At first it tries to avoid the flame, butting against the top of the jar, but as that space quickly fills with heat the hornet drops and bumps at the sides of the jar with the lazy swagger of a drunk. It flies into the candle once and then, as if blaming the candle for the collision, it flies at it again and again while the flame silently tongues at the air. After a moment the candle begins puffing black smoke into the jar, filling the air inside with twisting clouds that bind the hornet to the surface of the desk. At last the hornet stumbles aimlessly on the spot, paws at the wood in its death throes, and collapses beneath its own weight. It twitches its wings a few times before the flame wobbles and weakens and winks out in one last sputter of smoke. Nothing moves behind the glass any more.

Yet, I imagine, the silence is short. Another snarl enters the room from the doorway behind the girl. Her father is the first to look up. She turns around in her chair and follows his gaze. A second hornet sits at the top edge of the door and, beyond the door, three or four more hornets bumble through the house, swooping up and down and dragging a long clump of thin legs behind them. The ground trembles. Scrymgeour strides past the girl and steps out of the forbidden room. He stands in the middle of the house, surrounded now by another dozen hornets, and he turns to the window beside him. He swears beneath his breath, inviting the girl to join him. She rises from her chair and draws close to him to look outside. What awaits her is an ominous vision. Beneath the stormclouds that gather low overhead and smear the sky black all the way to the horizon, a thin line of orange haze radiates out from a wall of flames far off in the distance. The scene looks almost as if the sun has decided that today it will set in the east. Between the clouds and the dust, against an amber backdrop, an immense swarm of hornets chokes up the air. Buzzing and swirling with awesome aggression, enemies with one another and with the whole world around them, they rise and tumble across the land like the atomised smoke of the faraway fire.

There is a rational explanation for the arrival of the hornets here. According to the newspaper reports that appeared in the following days, that fire burned a path two hundred miles long from Idalia, just southwest of the Whangie, to the settlement of Orion far off in the southeast. That arc of wild bushland, which now comprises a scatter of national parks, is almost wholly rooted in the moist clay and mud that the Australian hornet, *Abispa ephippium*, uses to build its burrows and nests. When the fire raged through the bushland, it awoke all the hornets that were nesting at the time and drove them north as one. But then, beyond this rational explanation, there is a darker significance to the arrival of the hornets here. Every Aboriginal tribe in Australia identifies itself with a totem animal, an animal found in plenty on the territory claimed by the tribe. The Jiman and several neighbouring tribes were known as hornet people because the hornet bank of outback Queensland, the actual vein of bushland clay from which Hornet Bank derived its name, bisected the south of their tribal territory and even now provides a home to millions of those vicious insects. As hornet people, all of those tribes were self-appointed custodians of their totem animals. They were responsible for culling and cultivating the hornets however the season might require. They were also responsible for performing the ceremonies which would routinely flush the hornets out of the clay and the mud in order to increase their presence whenever the tribesmen felt moved to display their prowess before an attack. The inference to be drawn from all this is that, in my view, the fire that drove those hornets north was not a natural event. I think it was lit intentionally and controlled with expertise. I think those tribesmen had had enough of Scrymgeour and his acolytes, and I think they saw something they decided they could not abide. I think that the hornet trapped in that jar was the first whisper of a warning to the settlers at the Whangie, a warning that they had drawn to themselves the eye of a storm far more forbidding than the one then threatening to throw itself down from the sky.

That night, all night, is alive with hornets trapped in the corners of rooms, thrumming their wings and thudding themselves against the sides of the house. The girl is unable to sleep for the noise and for the sense that danger, once distant, has come to pollute the air around her. But when dawn fills the homestead with a rising heat that wearies the hornets out of their flight, the girl feels a pressing need to breathe in the open air and she steps out onto the wraparound porch only to freeze at the door. Although she cannot know it yet, what she sees is a danger more severe, more incendiary, than any danger those insects might pose. A young man stands at the hitching-post and watches her from beside his horse. He offers a wave of a hand bound in a kerchief, a bandage on a hornet bite he suffered during his ride to the Whangie. He wears the black trousers and vivid red coat of the British Imperial Army, although his clothes are soaked through from the overnight storm and are now steaming dry in the first warmth of day. He sports the tall, lean body of a middleweight boxer, a born combatant in any event, but the absence of a lame leg and a slight hunch is not enough to spoil the likeness he strikes with that jutting jaw and those deepsunk eyes. He forces a smile, without showing his teeth, when a look of mistrust flits across the girl's face. I try to imagine the turmoil in his mind at this encounter. I try to catalogue all the things he could say, but does not, for fear that lacklustre words will taint the power of the reunion. He might tell her how long it took him to ride here from Rockhampton. He might tell her how soon he came when he learned that she was living here, and he might add how appalled he was when he learned that she had been brought to this place. He might ask whether she received even one of the letters he wrote her in the first seven years of his absence. Finally, though, he steps towards her, the sweat beading on his brow even as the rain drips from his hair, and he speaks to her to allay her evident confusion. I don't expect you to recognise me after all this time, he says, but please don't tell me you've forgotten that we ever knew one another.

William Rowan Scrymgeour was born in Rockhampton in 1864. He was the first child and only son of Rowan and Emmeline Scrymgeour and, long after his death in the Sudan in 1898, he would become my great-great-grandfather. His son, Charles William Scrymgeour, was born in Rockhampton in 1892, and died at Passchendaele in 1917 as a volunteer infantryman in the First Australian Imperial Force. While stationed in Dunkerque in 1915, Charles Scrymgeour met Marion Davis, a nurse in the British Red Cross. Because Marion Davis died during the birth of her seventh child in 1933, I cannot know whether her relationship with Scrymgeour was founded on anything more than fleeting wartime lust. I know only that their time together resulted in the conception of a child, Victor, who was born at his grandparents' home in Lewes, Sussex, in 1916, a little less than a year before his father was killed. Victor Wentworth Davis Wood went on to become my paternal grandfather, taking his second surname from the man his mother later married, and it is through him and through Charles and finally through William that my father and I stand today as descendants of Rowan Scrymgeour, even though this account of Scrymgeour's life has been passed down to me through my mother and the elderly Abigail.

I admit I regret that these pages might diminish the role William played in the downfall of his father and the destruction of the Whangie. The bare facts are that William Scrymgeour arrived at the Whangie the day it was set alight and that he fled on horseback, with his sister, before the flames died down. I regret that he carries with him the taint of the magic bullet. I regret that the preceding narrative reduces his arrival to a sort of technical device, a convenient means of resolving the conflict between the girl and her father and bringing their story to a close. And I regret that those bare facts leave little room for texture and nuance, obscuring the larger role that I suspect he played in the chaos. I think there was nothing opportune or accidental about his being at the Whangie just before it burned. I think there is something more to his arrival, something concealed by the spectacle of his riding in to rescue his sister in the nick of time. I think it was no coincidence that he arrived at the Whangie so close to its end because I think he helped usher in its destruction when he decided to go there. More than saving his sister from the flames, William Scrymgeour seems to me to have unwittingly ignited the fire. He didn't just happen to be there when the homestead burned. The burning happened, in part, because he went there when he did.

In 1972, Abigail Scrymgeour captivated my mother with her recollections of the ambush on the Auchtermuchty Bend. It began with William's return, she said, and proceeded to an argument between the young man and his father. The drift of that argument is impossible to know, but I know enough about William to strike close to what I think is the truth. In 1878, when William Scrymgeour was fourteen years old, the Queensland colonial government passed the Volunteer Act which sought to swell the ranks of the colony's contribution to the Imperial Army. In 1880, when William Scrymgeour was sixteen years old and therefore of enlistment age, the outbreak of the First Boer War would have seen him sent to the Transvaal as soon as he signed up. According to enlistment records, however, William did not sign up until he was almost seventeen. He waited more than two hundred days from the date on which he became eligible before he volunteered for armed service, and, by the time he was enlisted, the Boer War had already come to an end. I know from William's later service that he was not a coward. I know, in fact, that he suffered from an irrepressible hunger to honour himself in battle. He received a Distinguished Conduct Medal for his service in the Third Anglo-Burmese War, and he remained active in Burma even after the insurgency was quashed in 1887. Following that, he opted not to retire and instead volunteered to serve in South Africa in 1893, in Ghana in 1895, and under the command of Lord Kitchener in the Sudan in 1896. He did not postpone enlisting because he was afraid of the Boer War. Just the opposite, I think. He wanted to fight in the Transvaal, I'm sure, but he felt obliged to inform his father before he took up arms. I think his father was out droving when the war erupted, and I think the war had ended by the time his father returned.

Rowan Scrymgeour could not have reacted gracefully to his son's desire to risk his life for the Crown. This is a man who had done everything in his power to escape the dictates of those in authority. He had freed himself from the yoke of his father-in-law and then, for a gruelling twenty-three years, he had endured a drover's life so that he might eventually take himself and his family to the farthest reaches of the Empire and beyond the eye of the Crown. I imagine him attempting to dissuade his son from signing up and, when that fails, I imagine him disparaging the boy's decision. The young man's mother stands at the window where she tries to soothe the two-year-old daughter made anxious by rising voices. The young man warns his father that he will not be owned by his parents, that his life is his alone to live, and I imagine that those words only inflame his father because they appeal so strongly to the man's own beliefs. The boy signs up the next day, kissing his mother before leaving home but finding himself rebuked by the father whose hand he tries to shake, and when he is gone, I imagine, Scrymgeour bundles up and destroys all his belongings except for some token items he retains in private. A pair of trousers and a white shirt, and the long black oilskin he had bought for the boy's sixteenth birthday. I suppose he had hoped that the two of them might someday go droving together. Now, his hopes dashed, he rests the clothes in a wooden chest which he stores away for safekeeping. The chest of clothes becomes, in effect, a private epitaph for the son he lost to the clutches of the Crown.

I imagine he does not even greet the boy when William presents himself at the Whangie. He stands behind the girl on the porch, hornets still crawling across the planks, and glares down at his son in the glow of dawn. What he sees before him is a Shadbolt in the making. This vision of the boy is not totally unjustified. Sometime in March 1890, just after William returned home from Burma, it was Shadbolt who sent the young man news of recent events at the Whangie and forwarded a copy of the newspaper portrait with which Scrymgeour proffered his daughter for marriage.

You, Scrymgeour whispers to his wet and weary child. Who do you think you are? This is not your home. You have no right to be here.

The boy is taken aback, startled by his father's hostility, but rather than merely retort he tries to gain the upper hand. No right? he says softly. No right? My mother lost her life here and has been buried on this land. Am I not allowed to visit her final resting place?

I imagine that Scrymgeour hesitates, unable to see how the boy could have known the fate of the woman whose bones lie in the ground, but rather than seizing the bait he advances and gives the boy a shock as good as the one he got. More fool you, he sneers. Your mother didn't just *lose* her life. She decided to *take* it.

This news comes as a blow to the boy and that blow is what sparks the skirmish. Their confrontation lasts the better part of an hour as the two men, increasingly loud, exchange and repeat and reiterate accusations and shout all the settlers out of their sleep. The boy condemns his father for driving his mother to madness and warns that he risks driving his sister to madness as well. The man insists that the boy knows nothing of his mother's state of mind because he chose to abandon her, to gallivant around the globe, instead of staying by her side to offer some support. He adds that the woman might still be alive if her son had chosen a different path. The boy declares his father a tyrant, a despot intent upon owning not just the things but also the people around him, and he berates him for selling his daughter into bondage under the guise of a marriage arrangement. The man laughs in his face and asks the boy what he will do to stop him. The boy tells him that sooner or later the world will serve him his just deserts. The man spits at the boy's feet. That's why I can no longer call you my son, he says. You won't use your own hands to shape the world as you want it to be. All you do is bend it according to other men's instructions, and when your commanders are nowhere to be found all you do is sit back and watch the world shape itself and hope, just *hope*, that the pieces resolve in a way that advances your interests. He sucks in his cheeks, swills up saliva, and leans forward to spit at the boy's feet again. At least your sister had the stomach to wreak havoc on what I have built out here. She destroyed supplies and endangered stock and even descended into the muck for no other reason than to spite me. You are your mother's son. You are a woman at heart. This girl is more man than you'll ever be. Scrymgeour sneers at the boy standing before him, then raises his arm and extends a finger and points down the slope to the river. But go on, he says, if you must. You'll find a small cairn marking the spot. Go and pay your respects if you like, then turn around and be gone from here.

The ambush began when William Scrymgeour followed the first of his father's commands but refused to follow the second. I see him return from the grave to the Whangie. The light of late morning throws a tawny haze across the land. William sets his jaw, I imagine, and stares hard at the vicious old man. You are an abject beast, he says, if you suppose there's humour in this. But the old man's confusion, an involuntary frown, tells William that what he just saw by the river was not of his father's doing. William offers an explanation that produces a panic in Scrymgeour. There's nothing at that cairn, he says. That grave is open and empty.

Scrymgeour limps harder the quicker he tries to stride down the path to the water's edge. He leaves the boy and the girl behind him as he stomps towards the beckoning grave. This will emerge as his first fatal mistake. Stuck by the river at the base of the slope, he will have nowhere left to turn when he finds himself under attack. When he reaches the grave he discovers the cairn destroyed, the stones scattered across the mud, and the resting place transformed into a raw pit dug apparently with human hands. Footprints, hundreds of them, surround the hole. Scrymgeour peers inside. The bones have been removed. The empty grave opens wide like the maw of some muddy beast. I see the panic on his face evolve into outright fear. I see him wanting to scream out, wanting but not knowing what to scream out, and I see him suddenly paralysed by the alien sensation of indecision. This will emerge as his next fatal mistake. Overcome by the shock of the empty grave, he will waste precious time trying to interpret the meaning of this spectacle rather than seeking safety. I see him grasping at the implications of the mess before him. The tribesmen were here, on his land, in uncountable numbers and under cover of darkness. They had taken care to keep quiet. They had known exactly where to find the most sacred site on the property. They had planned this carefully. But then, in hindsight, I am able see what Scrymgeour never could. When I look above him and over his head, I can see his enemies preparing to strike.

The girl watches her father from the safety of the porch and then senses something, a presence, atop the towering Auchtermuchty Escarpment. She fixes her eyes on its rocky rim, beyond the black birds high in the air, and there she catches a glimpse of a movement made in stealth. After a moment a man steps forward and then, in his wake, a dozen more emerge. Each of these men wields an enormous spear and each one glows almost ochre in the late morning light. They gather, slowly, on the edge of the rocky rim, and peer over it and down at where Scrymgeour loiters nearly directly beneath them. The girl says nothing to her brother beside her. The girl decides to say nothing to him. William spies the men just a second later, but a second is all it takes for them to gain the advantage. He dredges a cry from the depths of his stomach. His father's name hits the air in the same instant as the first spear. Rowan Scrymgeour has just turned back to look up at his son on the porch when, as if pierced by a bolt of lightning come screaming out of a pristine sky, he feels his face smash into the marl and tastes the tang of blood in his mouth and tries to right himself, on instinct, only to fall again when he feels a sharp bite deep in the thick of his thigh. He cranes his head up from the dust over which he has spattered his blood and he peers up the slope at his children. All he can see is the placid face of the girl looking back at him as her brother sweeps her into his arms and runs.

What thoughts must have bombarded Scrymgeour when he felt himself fall to the ground? Was he kicked off-kilter by the speed and shock of the attack? When he woke that morning in the first pale light, the day seemed to promise a routine as tedious as any other.

He lay there on his straw bed in the gathering warmth, I imagine, and he thought of nothing more than setting out to milk the cows. Now look at him. A son returned from an eight-year absence and the promise of death at the hands of black brutes and still it is not yet time to partake of a midday repast. Did he wonder how they had orchestrated the ambush without attracting his attention? Did he puzzle over the logistics of it and attempt to identify his weaknesses? Did it enrage him further to know that the roles had been reversed as he now fell victim to the malevolent schemings of others? Or did he think of the day ahead? Did he think of the ways he might survive it? Did he think he might quell the attack somehow and still find time to milk the cows?

I can't help but feel that he might have felt a sneaking admiration for his enemies, for those who carried out the attack as well as those who enabled it, if only he had survived long enough to reassemble the chain of events as I feel it must have unfolded. I admit that what I am about to write is almost entirely conjecture. Beyond imagining what it was like for someone to experience actual events, I now imagine the events themselves in an effort to fill the spaces between certain recorded facts. Oblique and incomplete documentation invites, at this point, a speculative leap. Here are the facts as documented. The evening of the day on which Shadbolt, Watlington, and the three other horsemen rode out to the Whangie and were repulsed by Scrymgeour, the party returned to Jericho where Shadbolt filed two reports. The first report recounts the attempt to add the names of the men at the Auchtermuchty Bend to the military register of the colony of Queensland and it makes note of the threat of armed insurrection if registration were to proceed. The second report reveals that, on their way back from the Whangie, Shadbolt and Watlington sighted a mob of between sixty and eighty Aboriginal tribesmen slowly heading west on foot. I imagine the horsemen pressing on through the endless dust when the tribesmen appear on the horizon like a dark lowlying cloud. I imagine the electric nervousness, the staying of the horses, the tribesmen standing stockstill when the strangers approach and confront them. There, then, is the reported sighting. Now I must imagine more than what was later written down.

Watlington dismounts his horse and carefully, carefully approaches the tribesmen. The remaining riders, including Shadbolt, are made anxious by his venture, but Watlington proceeds through the dust to draw in close to his people. From the mob of tribesmen an elder emerges, a lank and longlimbed old man with a grey beard wisping down to his chest. The elder intercepts the Native Policeman before Watlington reaches the rest of the tribe and, meeting midway between their respective parties, the two men enter into an exchange of words. The elder clearly does not trust Watlington and probably does not want to trust him, but I imagine that Watlington offers him information he cannot simply ignore. I have seen the bones of your missing boy, Watlington whispers in a dialect they share. The bones have been stripped and desecrated by a settler who is at this moment assembling his own little army with which he will decimate the rest of your men. I wish I could say why Watlington spoke to the elder about what he saw and knew. Did he harbour some hope, somewhere deep inside, that he might make amends with the kinsmen he oppressed if he sacrificed Scrygmeour to their vengeance? Or was he an unswerving servant of the Crown, an underling who cherished his allegiance so devoutly that he leapt at this opportunity to eradicate the brazen bastard who mocked it? Or might he have found a way to respond to his suspension between those two worlds at war, enticing his black enemies to strike at his white enemies and then taking a step back to watch his adversaries bleed one another? I am not able to say for certain. Cold, hard, and stoic in all his surviving portraits, Watlington remains impenetrable to me. All I can do is imagine, here, that the deaths of dozens of desperate settlers were sealed with whispers in the desert as two inaccessible men, each with motives I cannot understand, united in a chance encounter and plotted their destruction. Of course it's possible that

no such encounter ever took place and that the tribesmen attacked the Whangie the next day for reasons
only they can know. But Shadbolt and Watlington
did see those tribesmen, and Watlington had seen the
bones of the boy, and within twenty-four hours the
tribesmen had razed the settlement in which those
bones were kept. On top of that, Watlington had spent
weeks surveying the Auchtermuchty Bend, and the
tribesmen who razed it carried out their offensive with
the sort of military precision that would surely require
the advice of a surveyor. If it's the case, as I fear it may
have been, that the tribesmen thereafter glimpsed
William Scrymgeour bound for the Whangie in uniform, that sighting would have added ballast to what
Watlington said to the elder. William's arrival would
have dovetailed with the suggestion that Scrymgeour
was preparing to make war on the natives he despised
and, in fact, it likely would have led them to rouse
those hornets with a fire lit in a build-up to battle.

When the tribesmen at last arrived at the Whangie
and William Scrymgeour fled, he did not flee the
fight because he was terrified by it. He was a soldier
whose familiarity with military strategy allowed
him to see the coordinated precision of the ambush.
I watch him watch the spear drop down to fell, but
not kill, the old man at the grave, and I imagine he
understands how the ambush will unfold before his
father even hits the ground. The dust around the

Whangie remains untouched by the footprints of the tribesmen. They could not have defiled the grave after approaching it on land. They must have taken a dugout canoe, or an armada of dugout canoes, and ridden the river all the way to the Whangie from some point south of the Auchtermuchty Bend. They must have disembarked at the tip of the inland peninsula and defiled the grave before ascending the escarpment. The defilement was a lure, of course, but so too might be the man's wounding there. If he were to scream, he would immediately attract the attention of all the other settlers. If there were more tribesmen than those atop the escarpment, if some had disembarked and dispersed throughout the settlement, the settlers would emerge into daylight and converge by the river like cattle lumbering downhill to slaughter. They might be killed when they stepped out of their dwellings or they might rush to aid the fallen man and then be killed from above. William watches an agonised grimace twist at his father's face. Quickly he turns to his sister and gathers her up in his arms and bolts for his horse at the hitching-post.

The girl locks her eyes on her father downhill and does not flinch from the suffering he endures. He summons breath and rage from the deepest reaches of himself and unleashes an almighty scream that resounds throughout the settlement. The girl jolts in her brother's arms and feels his thundering heartbeat where he holds her against his chest. From this distance, I imagine, she can see the other settlers alive and called to assist and stumbling out of their half-built homes. Then, I imagine, she sees the dark shapes of tribesmen bearing weapons as they stream in from the north and the south and flood across the Bend. As their bare feet beat against the barren earth they summon up a pall of dust that obscures their distinguishing features and reduces them to shadows. Some of the settlers are slaughtered with a single swipe of a blade. Others are bludgeoned to death with clubs while their wives are run through with spears. A few settlers manage to evade the tribesmen, or perhaps they do not see them, and they rush down to where Scrymgeour lies screaming before they feel themselves at the mercy of the phalanx behind them. The girl is thrown onto the back of the horse. Two or three tribesmen, partway down the path, spin around as if to dart back and seize her, but by the time they see her passing the homestead she is already out of their reach. William has hauled himself into the saddle and spurred the horse to mount an escape. He rides eastward on raging hooves that kick dust over the tribesmen who fly up the path and leap onto the wraparound porch of the Whangie. Behind him the homestead thunders, a living thing enraged, as the tribesmen swarm in through the door to seek out what awaits them inside the forbidden room. While her brother sweeps the two of them out into the empty desert, the girl, looking back, watches the Whangie quiver and recede.

What lies ahead of them now is Jericho. Upon arrival, just after midday, William will report the ambush and summon a party of men enthused by the prospect of bloody reprisals. The machinery of retribution will kick into gear and in less than a fortnight Scrymgeour's allies will have claimed at least one hundred and twenty-seven lives. What lies beyond that, for the girl, is a return to Rockhampton that will last her the remainder of her childhood years. William will provide for her at first, for a year or so, until he marries a woman named Lydia Arnold with whom he fathers his son, Charles, in 1892. When he then volunteers to serve in Africa and moves his family to Cape Town, the girl will be sent to St Joseph's Orphanage in Neerkol, fifteen miles west of Rockhampton, and will leave there at age sixteen to accept a position as a maidservant on a colonial estate in Gladstone. She will lose contact with Lydia Scrymgeour following William's death in 1898, although Lydia's own death in 1912 will leave Charles effectively orphaned at twenty years of age with Abigail Scrymgeour his only next of kin. At the end of the First World War, after Charles' death at Passchendaele, Abigail will inherit the military pensions of both her brother and her nephew and she will use those funds to purchase the small home in Lutwyche in which she will greet my mother in 1972. By then she will have sleepwalked through federation and provided only scant support to the women's textiles initiatives of the First and Second World Wars, and, of course, she will have declined a request to comment on the unveiling of the statue of her father the year before. In 1977, she will pass away at home in her sleep.

Flames have sprung up from all of the buildings. Screams burst out of the last survivors. The girl cannot see her father but I imagine she imagines herself by his side in his moment of dying. He presses his face into the dust and writhes against the terrible spear like an insect pinned to a board. Blood stains the marl. Dirt churns into the gash in his leg. He looks up the slope, struggling to see his children, when he hears the screams of the dying settlers and then sees more tribesmen, too many more, emerging from the wheat-field and from amongst the cattle and from behind almost every blazing building. A dozen at first, then two dozen, five dozen, and more. Two black men for every settler. The settlers never stood a chance. He raises his eyes to the sky and then achingly turns on his side to see the men who have struck him. They stand on the ridge peering down. Each of them carries a spear except the one who launched the first strike. The spears leap skyward in unison and then, arcing, they start to drop. They whip through the air on their way down. What might be the last thought to teeter into

Scrymgeour's mind? He didn't even get the chance to utter some final words. He didn't even get the chance to look his attackers in the eye or to rise to his feet, pick up his weapon, and take the fight to them. He wants a moment more, just a moment longer, to make a final stand. He wants to strike the final blow and to utter the final word. He wants to punish, he wants to devour, whoever it is who would dare to reduce his empire to ash.

The statue was unveiled on June 18, 1971, outside the council offices of the small town of Jericho in the deserts of central Queensland. It remains there now, twenty-two miles east of where Scrymgeour built the Whangie and a little over a century after the settler was slaughtered and the homestead burned. The story the statue commemorates is a very simple one. On April 29, 1890, Rowan Scrymgeour was killed at the Auchtermuchty Bend along with his resident documentarian and nine settler families whose deaths accrued a body count of approximately forty-five. On May 10, 1890, the Colonial Police Force in Jericho reported the deaths of almost three times as many Aboriginal tribesmen killed in retribution for the ambush. Yet the statue of Scrymgeour glosses over that later story. The plaque beneath the statue identifies Scrymgeour as simply a local entrepreneur and only implies his premature end, aged fifty-nine, in the numerals that now encapsulate his lifetime: 1831–1890. Towards the beginning of these pages, I wrote that what compels me to articulate Rowan Scrymgeour here is the total, deceptive effacement of his complexities in the one representation of him that exists today. Those words have lost none of their truth. The statue leaves me disturbed and dismayed. It captures Scrymgeour's broadest features but omits the qualities that make him *worth* capturing. Arriving at the end of these pages, however, I worry that I have fared no better, that these words carry similar flaws, even as I also worry that I have articulated Scrymgeour with far more success than I can feel comfortable claiming.

Having hoped to make amends for a failure of the sculptor's imagination, I see now that my work is shot through with more failures than I can possibly count. These failures are as endemic to what I have written as they are to the people I have written about. George Scrope failed to imagine that the backbreaking poverty of Aloysius Scrmygeour might leave his son-in-law inclined to deceive and exploit him. Emmeline Scrymgeour failed to imagine that her husband might have seen her as a mere accessory to a life of greater comfort than his own, and William Scrymgeour failed to imagine that his father might have his reasons for antipathy towards armed service in the interests of the Crown. Rowan Scrymgeour failed to imagine that the boy he killed might have meant something profound to those who raised and nurtured him, and he failed to fully imagine that his brutality might incite them to seek retribution through slaughter. Ernest Shadbolt failed to imagine that his longtime ally might resent the absorption of his little empire into the sovereign territory of the Crown, and the sculptor whose work now stands in Jericho failed to imagine that his subject might have been less distinguished and regal than the hero he cast in bronze. From the day Scrope and Scrymgeour came together in Glasgow to the day Scrymgeour caught a spear in the thigh and several more in the torso, the chain of events was marked by the repeated failures of the people caught up in it to cast their minds into the lives of others and to imagine, really imagine, what sort of interests those others might harbour on the basis of their life experiences.

Looking back, though, I see my own imaginings of their lives pockmarked with any number of blind spots that leave these pages marred by a series of similar failures. I imagine the death of that young boy strung up on the hitching-post but I find myself unable to imagine the features of his face. I cannot imagine why he might have ventured out to the Whangie alone at night. I cannot decide whether he felt some thrill or some hint of imminent glory at the prospect of burning it down by himself or whether he felt trepidation and terror at having strayed off course while wandering the land. I sense these possibilities on the

periphery of recorded events but I cannot bring myself
to bring them to life. I can't imagine the boy's mother
and I can't say whether she was distraught or only puz-
zled when she woke the next day and failed to see her
son nearby, and I cannot inflame within myself the
fury and the thirst for justice that must have driven
his tribe to avenge him. I cannot adequately envision any of the indigenous men and women touched
by the events of this narrative, and I cannot hope to
empathise with them so as to evoke their experiences.
I can barely fasten a grip on Shadbolt, Watlington, and
Culvahouse, all of whom I have seen peering out from
dustflecked and faded ferrotype portraits. I can't gain
so much as a foothold on those who never made a real
bid for posterity or those who have become lost in the
labyrinth of the archives. My efforts to make amends
for an imaginative failure have only exposed the limits
of my own imagination and called forth bygone men
and women to gather together beyond its reach.

Yet I worry that the very urge to imagine events in
their totality, to collect and absorb and comprehend all
the facts and then to attempt to convey them in words,
is a sort of unconscious gesture that plunges me further
into the shadow of an ancestor I cannot escape. I worry
that these pages are driven by a yearning to chronicle
every detail in the history of the Whangie and to corral
and coerce all those details into a narrative form, and I
worry that this yearning is a symptom of a compulsion

towards control and domination which I have inherited from Rowan Scrymgeour. I confess that this worry first came to me before I began writing these words. I quietly took a seat at my desk and reflected on my visit to the Auchtermuchty Bend. Under assault from a brutal sun, I had taken a walk alongside the river and wandered into the space where Scrymgeour's wheat once grew, and there, at a standstill, I looked out at the dust and I resurrected the wretched settler. Not in the thick of outrageous events. Not entangled with the girl, not plotting against or persecuting his indigenous enemies. An ordinary day brings with it an ordinary day's work on the farm. As the sun slowly arcs into the west, it edges the shadow thrown by the escarpment up and over the eastern slope and towards where I stand with my ancestor. He wields a scythe, both hands on the snaith, and slashes away at the bristling wheat. He proceeds methodically, bent at the waist with his hat on his head, and steadily carves a path through stalks that rise to shoulder height. Suddenly, though, he stops. He slows to a halt as if struck by a thought and he raises his eyes from the ground beneath him. The brim of his hat recedes from his brow and peels its shadow away from his eyes. Those deepsunk eyes look up at me but pierce straight through me as if I'm a ghost. Scrymgeour stands before me, breathing hard but otherwise unmoving, and allows himself a moment to indulge in what seems a daydream. What is it, in his mind's eye, that has arrested him so? Standing there and watching him, a tingle travels the length of my spine. Recalling that tingle as I sat at my desk, I reached for the nearest scrap of paper and on it I scribbled a note that I find disquieting even now: 'I imagine Scrymgeour imagining me'.

I imagine Scrymgeour imagining me. I imagine him embarking on a day's labour more than a century ago and channelling into his every movement visions of an inland empire peopled by his own descendants. I imagine him satisfying the pitiless demands of farm-work in the desert and justifying his sweat, his sunburn, and his aching muscles with his anticipations of a future in which this land may yet shelter and sustain his children, his children's children, his children's children's children and on and on forever. I imagine him imagining me. I imagine him seeking refuge in a quiet moment and casting his thoughts as far ahead as they will go in order to picture his progeny in generations still to come. I imagine him imagining the sorts of qualities he hopes to pass down, the resilience and the resourcefulness and, above all, the infinite patience.

I wonder, then, what he would make of me if he could see me standing before him and attempting to channel into words the substance of his life. My own life, I admit, is marked by a history of scattershot ambitions and of abuses and deceptions and minor triumphs eked out at extraordinary cost to myself and to those who stood in my way. That history rarely elicits feelings of pride when I look back on it now. Would it make my ancestor proud? Would he see my more ruthless actions as somehow necessary to my endeavours? I carry his blood in my veins. Do I carry something more in my heart? Have I sometimes shown myself to be the sort of man he would have wanted me to become? I suppose I want to know how much of myself belongs to Rowan Scrymgeour, and how much of Rowan Scrymgeour survives today in me. But of course this can't be known, this knowledge simply cannot be had. Bequeathed the urge to exert control that drives me now to contain him in words, I find him still thwarting my every effort and twisting away from each turn of phrase intended to pin him down. Scrymgeour evades all articulation to lurk in the whiteness surrounding these words, and worse, when failure tempts me to stop and simply start afresh, I sense him already waiting for me in the whiteness of any new page I may ever hope to write.

ACKNOWLEDGEMENTS

Many existing studies of the frontier wars in colonial Queensland were instrumental in my efforts to accurately represent the historical context in which Rowan Scrymgeour lived and died. Prime amongst these studies was Gordon Reed's *A Nest of Hornets* (1982), the definitive account of the Hornet Bank massacre and its aftermath. Also valuable were Jonathan Richards' *The Secret War* (2008), L.E. Skinner's *Police of the Pastoral Frontier* (1975), and Raymond Evans, Kay Saunders, and Kathryn Cronin's *Race Relations in Colonial Queensland* (1975), all of which offer insightful accounts of the establishment and conduct of the Queensland Native Police Force. For more general details on the violence, politics, and legacy of the frontier wars, Henry Reynolds' *The Other Side of the Frontier* (1981), Ross Gibson's *Seven Versions of an Australian Badland* (2002), and Raymond Evans'

A History of Queensland (2007) were indispensable.
Rodney Sturges' *A Bibliography of George Poulett
Scrope: Geologist, Economist, and Local Historian*
(1984) provided many of the details on the British
aspects of Scrymgeour's story, as did Scrope's own
Principles of Political Economy (1833). The public and
academic institutions whose archival materials made
my research possible have been acknowledged where
appropriate in the text, as have the individuals through
whom Scrymgeour's story was transmitted to me.

My deepest gratitude to my wife, Marnie, for her
unwavering support during the writing of Blood and
Bone; to my editor, Emily Stewart, for all the advice
and assistance with which she helped make this book
the best it could be; and to Seizure, Xoum, and the
Copyright Agency, for the vital support they offer to
writers and readers of new Australian literature.

www.ingramcontent.com/pod-product-compliance
Lightning Source LLC
Chambersburg PA
CBHW051251250626
47155CB00009B/3251